Nutcracker Sweets at Moonglow

NUTCRACKER SWEETS AT MOONGLOW

A Moonglow Christmas Novella

DEBORAH GARNER

CRANBERRY COVE PRESS

Cranberry Cove Press / Published by arrangement with the author

Nutcracker Sweets at Moonglow by Deborah Garner

Cranberry Cove Press
PO Box 1671
Jackson, WY 83001, United States

Library of Congress Catalog-in-Publication Data Available
Garner, Deborah
Nutcracker Sweets at Moonglow / Deborah Garner—1st United States edition
1. Fiction 2. Woman Authors 3. Holidays

p. cm.
ISBN-13:
978-0-9969960-6-8 (paperback)
978-0-9969961-1-2 (hardback)

Printed in the United States of America
10 9 8 7 6 5 4 3 2

For my mother,
who always made holidays special for us.

ONE

"Where will we put them?"

Mist sat at the kitchen's center island, the reservation book spread before her. Betty's question was a good one. The Timberton Hotel was almost full, as was usual for the holidays. If not for a recent cancellation by a small group from Omaha, there wouldn't be any rooms available at all. As it was, there were only three.

"We can manage," Mist said, studying the room chart. She reached across the wooden surface and touched Betty's hand gently, reassuring the hotel owner. "The mother and daughter can stay in Room 16, one of the two men can go in Room 22, and the other can take Room 24.

Betty paused, and then nodded. "There's only one bed in Room 16, but it's a good-sized room. Clive could bring over that roll-away he has stored in the back of his gallery."

"That's what I was thinking, too," Mist said. "The daughter is only ten years old, so I think that will work. Yes, we'll make it work."

"It's such an unfortunate situation." Betty sighed and shook her head. "Having that theater burn down right before Christmas? And now, with flights booked solid, they're stuck for the holidays, away from home."

"We'll make this feel like home for them, then," Mist said, a soft smile crossing her face. If not for her calm demeanor, she might have looked impish.

"Like you do for our holiday visitors every year, dear," Betty said. "If anyone can create a home-away-from-home, it's you."

Mist stood up and closed the reservation book. "Thank you, Betty, but we all work together to make this a holiday home for our guests." She adjusted the sleeves of her oversized wool sweater and brushed off the front of her heavy cotton skirt, an old-fashioned print that she'd taken a fancy to at the local thrift shop.

"So we'll have the cast members, as well as a mix of new and returning guests," Betty said. "That's a full house, not to mention the annual cookie exchange, and your famous Christmas Eve meal. It sounds like we have our work cut out for us this year."

"It's not work when we're spreading joy," Mist said. "Especially at this time of year, and with such a unique mixture of guests." She moved to the sink, filled a kettle with water, and put it on the stove to heat. "Herbal tea?"

"Yes," Betty said. "I just made a pot of coffee, but I drank my fill of it this morning. A cup of tea sounds more soothing."

"Peppermint, cinnamon-apple, lemon-ginger or?" Mist left her question open-ended as she opened a canister on the counter and pulled out a variety of tea bags.

"What did you fix last night?" Betty asked. "It was delicious." She turned as the back door opened.

"Ah." Mist smiled. "That was hibiscus, with just a touch of lemon and honey."

"That sounds …" Betty's comment was cut short by a hearty laugh.

"Absolutely boring! Can't a guy get a plain old cup of coffee around here?"

Both Betty and Mist smiled at Clive's typical entrance. If it wasn't something cooking that brought the gallery owner around, it was a craving for fresh-brewed coffee - aside from his desire to see Betty, of course. Any excuse was good enough for a visit to his favorite lady.

"I just happen to have coffee on the menu today," Betty said, chuckling. "But you might think about trying something new now and then."

Clive put his arm around Betty's shoulders and gave her a peck on the cheek. "It sounds like you've been hanging around some mysterious California transplant, picking up some of her new age habits." He winked at Mist. "Isn't that what you call it: new age? Makes it sound like we're in the future or something."

Mist set Clive's favorite coffee cup on the center island. "That's because it *is* the future, Clive. We're always in the future."

"Uh oh," Clive said as he took a seat. "Here is comes, a dollop of Mist philosophy." He winked again, this time at Betty.

"The future is simply a bridge to the present," Mist said. She removed the tea kettle from the stove and poured a cup of tea for Betty, as well as one for herself. Bringing both cups over to the center island, she took a seat. Betty filled Clive's mug with coffee and sat down next to him.

"All ready for this year's holiday guests?" Clive asked.

"Yes and no," Betty said. "We've had some last minute changes."

"Oh?" Clive raised his eyebrows as he took a sip of coffee and glanced between Betty and Mist.

"Just a few more guests to make the holidays merrier," Mist said.

Betty nodded. "A few of the cast members from the Sapphire Ridge Theatre will be staying with us."

"Ah," Clive said. "I heard about the fire there. Terrible. They had to cancel the rest of the Nutcracker shows, didn't they?"

"Yes," Betty said. "Fortunately, we're shuffling a few rooms around and will be able to have them stay with us."

"That'll be a full house, then," Clive said. "Even more than usual. You have some returning guests this year, don't you? I know Michael will be here." He winked at Mist. It wasn't a secret that Mist and Michael had continued to grow closer during the past year.

"Just short of overflowing," Betty said. "Yes, Michael will be here, and the professor will be back, as well."

"How about new guests?" Clive took another sip of coffee.

"A family," Mist said. "Two parents and a young daughter."

"Right," Clive said. "The child we set up the ramp for?"

"Yes," Mist said. "She'll be in a wheelchair. The father said he could carry her up the front steps to the hotel, especially since there are only a few. But the ramp will offer an option. They'll have a room on the first floor, so she'll be able to get around easily once inside."

"The professor will stay upstairs," Betty said. "So will Michael, the cast members from the show, and …" Betty's voice trailed off as she looked at Mist for clarification on the guest's name.

"Ms. Olga Savinova," Mist said. "Another new guest. She'll be traveling alone. I believe she's older, from her voice on the phone. She had a slight accent, as well - Russian, I would guess from her name, though her address is in New York. I'm giving her a first floor room because she mentioned a knee problem."

"She's arriving this evening." Betty said. "A few guests are."

""Yes," Mist said. "The Rivera family will be here around nine p.m. They have a late flight into Bozeman." She checked the notes in the reservation book. "Luisa and Rafael are the parents. Maria, their ten-year-old daughter, is the one who will be in the wheelchair."

"The rest of the guests will be arriving tomorrow," Betty said. "At least I think so. Michael Blanton and Nigel Hennessy are driving down together from Missoula now that they both teach at the university there."

"Ah, yes," Clive said, grinning. "I know someone is especially glad that Michael took that open teaching position."

"They might try to make it tonight," Mist said. "Otherwise they'll be here in the morning." She tried her best to ignore Clive's teasing, but smiled in spite of the attempt.

Clive finished his coffee and stood up. "Well, you two lovely ladies just let me know what I can do to help, and I'll be glad to lend a hand."

"Now that you mention it, we were hoping to borrow that extra roll-away you have," Betty said. She turned on her most charming smile.

"Absolutely," Clive said. "I'll bring it over this evening. I'd better get back to the gallery. Speaking of which," he added, directing his comment to Mist, "I could use more of your miniature paintings. They're selling as quickly as my jewelry. You wouldn't happen to have any of the ones with the gingerbread house surrounded by pine trees, would you?"

"I have a few more of those ready, plus several with the winterberries," Mist said. "I'll drop them off when I pick up the fresh greenery I ordered from Maisie. I'm going by her place later this afternoon."

"Great," Clive said. "And I'll get that bed over here right after the gallery closes tonight." He gave Betty another quick peck on the cheek, and headed out.

Mist and Betty exchanged amused looks after Clive left. The phrase, "right after the gallery closes," might just as well have been "right about dinner time."

"Sounds like I'd better get that pot roast in the oven," Mist said.

"I'd say so." Betty laughed.

TWO

Mist glanced upward as she reached for the door handle to Maisie's Daisies. From the looks of the sky, it wouldn't be long before snow began falling softly on the small Montana town. Mist smiled. A snow-covered landscape was always welcome during the holidays. It added to the serene scene that Mist envisioned for the hotel guests.

Maisie looked up from a cluster of red carnations, white mums and holly branches when Mist stepped inside the shop. She wore a white thermal pull-over sweatshirt and denim overalls, and sported streaks of red and green hair mixed in with her natural color.

"Lovely," Mist said, eyeing the floral arrangement. "A customer order?"

Maisie shook her head. "No, this one's for us. Clayton's parents are coming to visit and I want something in the house to look like it might belong to grown-ups."

Mist smiled. Maisie and Clayton, the town's fire captain, had married a year and a half before and now had a six-month old son, Clay Jr. Their home was now filled not only with joy, but with an ample scattering of toys, stuffed animals, picture books, balls, building blocks, and a dinosaur-print baby blanket that could be found dropped in any random location around the house.

"I have your order ready for you," Maisie said, setting her personal project aside and fetching a large batch of greenery from the shop's back room. "Not much color this year, I noticed. You must have something unusual dancing around in that creative mind of yours."

"Yes, now that you phrase it that way," Mist said. "I've had something planned, but I'm going to sweeten it – so to speak - in view of a few additional guests we'll have. So perhaps the idea is 'dancing around,' as you say."

Maisie's face brightened. "Oh! You must have the Nutcracker cast staying with you! Clayton told me about the fire. A couple of the men from his fire crew went up there to help."

"We won't have the whole cast with us, just a few of them," Mist said. "One young girl and her mother, plus a couple of the men. The rest of the cast were either locals or found ways to get home."

"Well, the luckiest are the ones who'll be staying with you. Christmas at The Timberton Hotel is simply magical," Maisie said. "I'll be there to help you with Christmas Eve dinner, as always. I already warned our household. They can either come to the hotel or spend the evening at home together."

Mist nodded. "You do what's best for your family, Maisie, but I won't turn down the help if it really works for you, not with the full house we'll have."

"I wouldn't miss it," Maisie said, "even if only to see what you're going to do with all this." She removed the greenery from the tub, wrapped it in butcher paper, and tied twine around it. "Here you go. And here's your raffia, too." She handed Mist a small bag.

"Thank you, Maisie," Mist said. "What would I do without you?"

Leaving the rhetorical question lingering in the air, Mist slipped outside and headed to Clive's gallery, where she found Clive at his work table, hunched over a diminutive pendant in sterling silver. A Yogo sapphire sparkled under the overhead lights as Clive attached a tiny ring to the jewelry and slipped it onto a silver chain. He set the finished piece on a black velvet tray, alongside others.

"I love that teardrop design, Clive." Mist leaned forward and took a closer look. "I'm especially fond of the way each one is different, but has a similar sapphire somewhere in the design. Just as tears might fall differently from each other, yet find a way to sparkle in the end."

"Exactly what I was thinking," Clive said in a bright voice. He held a finger up in the air, as if just hit with a fabulous idea.

Mist laughed, well aware that he was teasing her. "Then again, maybe it's just a design that sells well."

"Even closer to what I was thinking," Clive said. "And speaking of what sells well ..." He raised his eyebrows and looked at Mist expectantly.

"Yes, I did bring you more paintings." Mist set the bundle of greenery and bag of raffia down on a chair and removed her backpack. She pulled out a half-dozen small bundles, all wrapped in cloth. She unwrapped each, saving the cloth for future use.

Clive nodded with approval. "Excellent. I'll display them on the front wall, next to Hollister's painting of the railroad trestle."

"It warms my heart that he's painting," Mist said as she walked over to admire the piece. The town's formerly homeless resident now lived in a room in the back of the hotel. Slyly, Mist had been slipping art supplies into his room for months. She'd seen him touch the supplies with longing, and knew it was only a matter of time before he gave in to the temptation of the blank canvas she'd mounted on his wall.

Mist returned to Clive's worktable, gathered the greenery and raffia into her arms, and headed for the front door. "Pot roast should be ready around six o'clock," she said casually.

"A welcome trade for the roll-away," Clive laughed.

Marge's candy store was conveniently located half-way back to the hotel. Mist's decorating endeavors didn't often include goods from Marge's shop. Aside from the previous year, when a gingerbread house needed to be decorated, a running supply of Betty's favorite caramels was the usual purchase. However, in view of the additional guests, Mist had decided to give into a whim and alter her plans for the café's buffet and table decorations. The greenery from Maisie's Daisies would make a perfect base. But her vision of the final arrangements required a hearty dose of sugar.

"Ah, there you are." Marge, a pleasant-looking woman of plump build and senior age, looked up from behind a tray of fudge as Mist entered. "I've got your order ready to go." She pulled a large bag down from a back shelf and placed it on the front counter. "I see your arms are full, though."

Mist set the bundle of greenery down on an ice-cream-parlor-style table, one of several available for customers. "Yes, but ..." She smiled as she removed her backpack and unzipped it, revealing an empty interior. "I just dropped off a few more paintings at Clive's gallery, so we can use this space."

Marge's face brightened. "I've been meaning to tell you how much I love your miniatures. Would you be interested in doing a custom order, some type of candy design?"

"A lovely idea," Mist said. "I'd be happy to. It's turning out to be a very sweet season. Then again, it's always a sweet season in here." She glanced around the interior of the shop. Large wooden barrels held salt water taffy, jelly beans, licorice ropes, and jaw breakers. Counter displays added chocolate truffles, nut clusters, and fudge squares to the mix.

Marge laughed. "Yes, you have a point there." She reached into the bag she'd packaged for Mist and removed several smaller packages, setting them on the counter. Mist's eyes lit up with delight.

"Wonderful," Mist said, picking up the first selection. "You found the old-fashioned ribbon candy."

"Yes," Marge said. "I was thrilled to get that in. It reminds me of my childhood. We always had a bowl of those on our living room table."

"Memories are part of the magic of the holidays," Mist said as she carefully placed the ribbon candy in her backpack. "They meander back and forth throughout our lives, at any time of the year. But they do seem to whisper a little louder at Christmas."

"Back and forth," Marge repeated. "Like the ribbon candy ..."

"Exactly."

"And these," Marge said, "I simply had to taste test. I'm sure you understand." She handed Mist a second package.

"Well, I can see why," Mist said. "We wouldn't want red raspberry filled hard candy that wasn't just right. You provided something very valuable, Marge: quality control."

"Happy to be of service," Marge said. An impish expression spread across her face. "The other hard candy flavors were delicious, too."

"I'm delighted to hear that," Mist said. "Thank you for helping with the last-minute order. Just put it on the hotel bill."

"No problem," Marge said. "Take a few of Betty's favorites to her, too." She slipped a few caramels into a bag and added them to the others.

One by one, Mist set the other packages – peppermint candies, honeycombed peanuts, thin mint wafers, chocolate-filled straws, and more – in her backpack, taking care to avoid breakage. As delicious as each variety sounded, her plans called for them to look as tantalizing as they tasted. Securing the sweet treasures on her back, she picked up the greenery, and returned to the hotel.

———

THREE

Mist stood in the doorway of the cafe, looking at the supplies she'd gathered. The greenery from Maisie's Daisies spread across the surface of an oak table like an elevated forest floor, rich in color and texture. Open packages of candy nearby sweetened the air with the aroma of sugar. A collection of antique mason jars stretched across the hotel's buffet table, reflecting beams of afternoon sunlight from the café windows.

"I can't imagine what you're going to create with from all that." Betty's voice floated out from the kitchen, behind Mist. "Not that I doubt you'll pull something fabulous together. You always do." A light clatter of dishes accompanied the comments. Mist had accepted Betty's offer to pull out dishes for the simple evening meal that would be served later on.

"It will create itself," Mist said softly. "I'm just waiting." It always worked that way. In time, the ideas formed, much the way a light breeze might begin on a late afternoon – unexpected, unannounced.

Approaching the buffet table, Mist picked up one of the mason jars and held it lightly, as if weighing it, and then lifted it, twisting it from side to side. She repeated the motion with several additional jars, all slightly different shapes and sizes, as if letting each one speak to her. She'd collected them for years, never with any particular intention, but knowing they'd be of use some day. The jars had fascinated her since she was a young girl, watching her grandmother prepare to can peaches. They represented endless possibilities - empty, yet inviting; limitless, though confined.

Now, Mist brought several jars to a table, and set the packages of candy from Marge's store alongside. She took a piece of red ribbon candy and set it in the bottom of one jar. Tilting her head, she looked at it from the side and adjusted the angle, so the curves of the sugary confection meandered in a way that pleased her. Nodding with approval, she chose another ribbon, a different color. Piece by piece, she filled the jar, creating a patchwork of colors and shapes that struck her as whimsical, yet soothing.

Peppermint sticks followed in another jar, and then chocolate-filled straws in yet another. Although some jars found themselves filled with assortments, many featured just one type of sweet. Many of the treats represented traditional Christmas colors, but not all. Just as the world was filled with contrast, Mist mused, so should art be. And décor was art, after all. Everything was art in one form or another.

In the end, a row of filled jars lined the buffet table from end to end, lids carefully screwed on. Mist examined the lengthy display, standing still a good five minutes. She then retreated to a storage closet, brought out two empty cartons, and loaded the jars inside.

"And ... where are those going?" Betty, now finished in the kitchen, had been watching as Mist packed the newly-filled jars away.

"In my room," Mist said calmly. She left with one box, returned for the other, removed it from the room, and returned again empty-handed.

"OK," Betty said. "And the greenery?" Her eyes glanced toward the table covered with holly branches, eucalyptus, and assorted evergreen boughs.

Again Mist disappeared, returning with a large bucket. She gently placed the assorted greenery inside the container and set it in a far corner of the café.

"OK," Betty repeated. Her expression grew more confused by the minute, especially when Mist came to stand by her side, looked around the room, and brushed her hands together as if everything were complete.

"And ..." Betty said.

Mist seemed not to hear at first, but then turned toward Betty. "And what?"

"And what will you be putting on the buffet and tables?"

"Do you mean tonight?" Mist asked.

Betty paused. "Yes, tonight."

Mist shrugged her shoulders. "Air," she said as she left the room.

* * *

The cafe in The Timberton Hotel was more or less the only place local townsfolk could get a decent meal. More specifically, there really was *no* place in town to get a "decent" meal. Residents of the town, as well as guests, could only choose one extreme or another. They could find a *less*-than-decent meal at Wild Bill's, down the road - where now, to everyone's relief, including his own, William Guthrie only served breakfast - or have an extraordinary meal at the Moonglow Café. Anything in-between would simply have to be fixed at home. And so, Mist's "simple" dinner for this particular evening consisted of a serve-yourself buffet of artisan breads and imported cheeses, pear and pomegranate salad, gnocchi with sage-butter sauce, pot roast with baby carrots and shallots, and Belgian chocolate gelato, kept cold atop a copper tub of ice. A small pitcher of caramel sauce sat beside the dessert service, for those who cared to spruce things up. The comparable translation for a "simple meal" was clearly "serve yourself."

The townsfolk who dined regularly at the café showed up in predictable order. Clayton arrived first with a couple of his fire crew. William "Wild Bill" Guthrie showed up a few minutes later. Millie, the town librarian, brought a visiting niece, settling in as the men in the café were midway through hearty portions from the buffet. Clive, as expected, rolled in just minutes after closing his gallery, spare bed in tow. Clayton took a break from eating to help Clive carry the roll-away upstairs to the appropriate room. When the two returned a few minutes later, Clive filled an overflowing plate and joined the firemen's table.

As per Mist's standard, but highly unusual, policy, the meal came without a set price, which always surprised newcomers. A small sign accompanied a pottery container near the café door, its elegant calligraphy simply stating "Pay what your heart tells you." Amazingly, the amount collected at the end of each day was more than enough to pay for preparing the next day's fare. Whether this was a result of small town generosity, appreciation of Mist's remarkable culinary skills, or relief over the now-defunct option of supper at Wild Bill's, no one knew. Rumor had it that William Guthrie often overpaid out of sheer gratitude at not having to eat his own cooking. Whatever the reason, it worked. Timberton locals remained well-fed, and visitors rejoiced in finding a culinary fantasyland.

"The Riveras called from Bozeman to say they'd be here in about an hour," Betty said as she put away the last of the dinner dishes.

"Perfect." Mist placed a cover on one of several leftover containers. "I just have a few final touches to add to the rooms. Otherwise, all the accommodations are ready, including those for tomorrow's arrivals."

"I'm not the least bit surprised," Betty said. "I'll refill the dish in the front hall while you do that. That dish seems to empty faster and faster every year!" Picking up the canister of glazed cinnamon nuts that she prepared each holiday season, she left the kitchen.

Mist stacked the leftover containers and took them to the spare refrigerator in Room 7, where Hollister would have easy access to them. Although he had become more comfortable in the presence of others, he still didn't come to the café for meals.

With the food safely tucked away, Mist moved to a closet in the downstairs hallway, and opened the door. Each shelf held various trinkets that she collected throughout the year. Often she had specific reasons for what she placed in each guest room. This year she'd decided to keep the small offerings random. Like life itself, she thought, unpredictable. Perhaps each item would be something that suited a particular guest's personality. Or perhaps it would strike a contrast in a unique way, reviving a long-forgotten memory, or planting the seed of a creative process.

Cradling a woven basket in one arm, Mist closed her eyes and reached onto shelves and into buckets and bins, grabbing whatever her fingers touched first. When the basket was filled, she closed the closet and moved from room to room, leaving an item – or two or three – on a dresser or nightstand. Taking care not to analyze the choices she pulled from the basket, she simply picked up whatever struck her fancy and left it behind as she traveled from one accommodation to the next. Once finished, she returned the basket to the closet, fixed herself a cup of herbal tea, and waited for the first guest to arrive.

FOUR

Olga Savinova was not exactly what Mist had expected, which struck her as odd, since she hadn't really had any expectations at all. In other words, the reality of the guest's presence in the hotel's doorway was different than a notion that she hadn't even had to begin with. At least that's the way she would have described the sensation, had she been asked. Those familiar with Mist's unusual way of thinking might have nodded quietly at this explanation, whether understanding it or not.

"Welcome to the Timberton Hotel, Ms. Savinova." Mist ushered the seventy-something woman in, and offered to take her coat, hat, gloves, and triple layers of scarves, each of which the guest peeled off slowly, while leaning on an exquisitely carved wooden cane. Her hand covered the curved portion of the crutch, obscuring its design.

"Thank you, dear," the heavy-set woman said, once relieved of the exterior trappings. Standing primly, grey hair fastened securely behind her neck, sapphire wool dress matching the color of her eyes, Olga Savinova looked nothing less than regal. She wore not a spot of make-up, as far as Mist could tell. A tiny brooch shaped like a swan adorned one shoulder.

"You must be tired from traveling," Mist said. "Would you like me to show you to your room? You can sign the registration card at your leisure."

"How kind of you," Olga said. "Yes, I do think I'd like to settle in."

"Right this way." Mist extended one arm toward the downstairs hallway, picked up the small suitcase, and then led the way. The woman followed behind, her cane tapping against the floor. Reaching the room, Mist escorted her inside, and indicated light switches, heater controls, and a door on a side wall. "This door goes to the next room, but is locked from both sides, so you'll have privacy, even though we have a full house. May I get something to drink? Tea, coffee, or maybe some hot apple cider?"

Olga shook her head. "No thank you. It's kind of you to ask, but I'd just like to rest now."

"Of course," Mist said as she stepped back into the hallway. "Just let me know if you need anything."

Mist had barely returned to the front lobby when the front door opened, and the Rivera family entered. The daughter, Maria, looked like an angel - petite, almost frail, with long, golden hair cascading forward over her shoulders. Her father held the handles of her wheelchair as he rolled her in. Her mother followed, stepping up to stand beside her once inside the entryway.

"Welcome to The Timberton Hotel," Mist said. "How was your trip here, Mr. and Mrs. Rivera, and … Maria, isn't it?" She leaned forward slightly to give the girl her own personal greeting. The young girl nodded and replied. "Yes, Maria."

"The trip was fine, but hectic," Mrs. Rivera said. "Airports are so crowded this time of year. And please call me Luisa. And this is Rafael." She turned and smiled at her husband.

"Do you need help with bags?" Clive asked as he stepped through the front door.

Rafael shook his head. "No, I can get them after we get situated. But thank you so much for the ramp."

"Yes," Luisa said. "Thank you. We knew there wasn't one here when we made the reservation, and we were fine with the front steps. You didn't need to do that."

"Nonsense," Clive said. "We like to do everything we can to make a visit comfortable for guests. Besides, what good are tools if they aren't used to build something now and then?"

"Absolutely," Betty said entering from the kitchen. "And tasks like that keep him out of trouble, too." She patted Clive affectionately on his shoulder.

Rafael laughed. "I believe I've heard similar comments around our house, as well." Luisa nodded her head while filling out the hotel registration card.

"Your room is ready for you," Mist said. "I could bring you coffee, tea, or other beverages, or you're welcome to help yourself anytime here in the lobby. The front parlor is open for relaxing, reading, or visiting with other guests."

"That sounds lovely," Luisa said. "I admit coffee sounds great about now. It's a little chilly here compared to our weather in Florida. We'll put our things away and come back out."

"Sounds like a task has been assigned," Rafael said to Clive. Both men picked up luggage and headed down the hall, Betty leading the way to the appropriate room.

"Do you have herbal tea?" Maria looked at Mist with a hopeful expression that seemed not only sweet, but angelic. "I especially love peppermint."

"It just so happens we have that," Mist said. "Sometimes it even comes with a stick of peppermint candy in it – on special occasions." She glanced at Laura for approval and was pleased when Maria's mother smiled and nodded. "And I think your arrival is a special occasion." Maria clapped her hands, delighted.

"Why don't we go get settled in," Luisa said. She set the completed registration card aside and stepped behind Maria's wheelchair.

"I can do it, Mom," Maria said. She placed her hands on the wheels with an attitude of independence that Mist found admirable.

"I'll show you the way," Mist said, beckoning the mother and daughter to follow her. Once inside the room, Mist pointed out the amenities, starting with the radiator. "This will keep you warm. It's not Florida, but it can be just as warm if the heat is high."

"Even better," Luisa said. "No humidity."

Mist smiled as a short conversation about muggy southern weather followed, but it wasn't the subject matter that caused the smile. New voices floating down the hall told her that two of her favorite guests had arrived. She excused herself politely and walked back to the front entryway. As she suspected, Michael Blanton and Nigel Hennessy stood near the registration counter. She reached out to shake Professor Hennessy's hand, and then extended the same gesture to Michael Blanton, causing all three to laugh.

"I dare say you can do better than that, my dear," the professor said, chuckling. "Your fondness for each other is not exactly a secret, you know." His charming British accent made his mock scolding even more amusing than the statement itself.

"I agree," Michael said. He took Mist's hand and pulled her gently toward him, bestowing a sweet kiss on her forehead, followed by a warm hug.

"Somewhat better, I suppose," the professor said.

Mist stepped back, assuming a proper hostess position, though with a soft blush on her face. "Your rooms are ready, of course, since Betty said you'd try to make it here tonight. And there's a nice fire going in the front parlor fireplace. So if you'd like to relax, or read, or have one of your famous literary conversations, just make yourselves at home." She handed both men keys to their rooms and indicated they could fill out registration forms at their convenience. As return guests, the hotel already had all their information.

"Truly, a spot of tea may be enough for me tonight," the professor said. "Grading papers is a weary task, and I'm quite ready for a good night's sleep."

"I just happen to have your favorite PG Tips tea," Mist said, knowing what the professor had enjoyed in the past. "I'll bring some up to your room along with some McVitie's digestives."

"Brilliant," the professor said. He checked the room number on his key and headed up the stairs with his luggage.

"Anything for you, Michael?" Mist said. "Tea? Coffee? Hot cocoa?"

Michael stepped closer to Mist and gave her a less reserved kiss than the one he'd given in front of the professor. "How about some quiet time with you in front of the fire? I'll get settled in my room and then come down to the front parlor."

"That sounds like a lovely plan," Mist said, smiling.

FIVE

Mist prepared the professor's tea and digestives and delivered them to his room. Knowing the other guests had turned in for the night, she quietly hung small bags of homemade cookies on their doorknobs and slipped a note under each door to let them know of the waiting treats. She returned to the kitchen to check breakfast preparations. Reassured that the morning meal was ready to go, she poured a mug of decaf for Michael, turned off all but one kitchen light and headed to the front parlor. As expected, she found Michael in his favorite chair by the fireplace, a stack of books in his lap.

"Quite the collection of Christmas books you have on display this year," Michael said as he held up one hardback copy. "*A Visit from Saint Nicholas*," he said. "Better known now as *The Night before Christmas*, of course. Did you know Clement Clark Moore originally published this anonymously in 1823? He didn't let it be known he'd written it until 1837."

"I didn't know that," Mist said, as she took a seat in the chair next to Michael's, a purple rayon skirt skimming the top of ballet flats. "That's why it comes in so handy to have a professor of literature around."

"You have two, you know," Michael pointed out. "Nigel is here, too."

"Perhaps we should hold a literature class while the two of you are both staying with us," Mist said. "But then, every day is a class. Life itself is filled with constant instruction."

"So true, especially when described in your Mist-type manner." Michael searched through other books in the pile. "I'm impressed. Harriet Beecher Stowe's *The First Christmas of New England*, O. Henry's *The Gift of the Magi*, Anthony Trollope's *Christmas at Thompson Hall*, and even Rudyard Kipling's *Christmas in India*."

"And don't overlook *The Grinch Who Stole Christmas*," Mist said. She lifted the popular Dr. Seuss book off a side table and added it to the rest of the stack.

"Of course," Michael said. "It wouldn't be Christmas without a children's tale."

"Children's tales are tales for *all* ages, you know." Mist said. "We're all children at heart, even more so during this time of year."

Michael set the books aside and reached for Mist's hand, folding it gently into his. "I've missed you. The Christmas holiday couldn't get here quickly enough this year."

Mist smiled. "I've missed you, too, Michael. However, I believe Christmas comes at the same time each year. There is no difference from one year to the next."

"Technically you're almost correct," Michael said.

"Almost?" Mist sat up in mock indignation.

"There are leap years, my dear Mist." Michael said. "Those add an extra day."

"Time is an ethereal concept to me." Mist let her free hand float in the air, as if skimming across water. "It flows continuously, so the distance from one Christmas to another is the same. It is simply the space between the two holidays." She rested her case by staring into Michael's grey-green eyes, admiring the unique color she'd labeled 'patina' the first time they'd met.

"There's no use in debating your view of the universe." Michael laughed. He kissed her hand and released it, as if admitting defeat. "Tell me about this year's guests. Are there any that I'll know, aside from Nigel? What about Clara Winslow and her gentleman friend?"

Mist shook her head. "Not this year, though they hope to be here next year. But we'll have a full house. Quite a few guests are here already – a nice family of three from Florida, and a woman from New York. They've turned in for the night already, after a long day of travel. Then we have you and the professor, of course. And others will be arriving tomorrow."

"Adults? Children?" Michael took a sip of decaf and waited politely for whatever information Mist felt proper to give.

"Both. Quite an interesting group, I suspect, very last-minute bookings," Mist explained. "A theatre not far from here burned down a few days ago. Several cast members could not get flights home after their show was cancelled, so they'll be spending Christmas with us. A mother and daughter, plus two other cast members."

"You'll have a full house, indeed," Michael said. "Or a full hotel, I should say."

"A full *home*," Mist whispered, as if telling a secret.

"Yes, a good point," Michael said. "The Timberton Hotel becomes home to anyone who steps inside, especially at Christmas."

"And that ..." Mist said as she stood up, "is not entirely by chance. Which reminds me that I still have work to do."

"At night?" Michael tried unsuccessfully to hide his disappointment, though it was moderated with a grin.

"Yes, even at night." Mist stepped around behind his chair and placed both hands on his shoulders. She leaned forward just close enough to whisper in his ear. "Night is often when the magic begins."

Leaving Michael to enjoy the warmth of the fire, Mist fixed herself a cup of chamomile tea in the kitchen and slipped into the back hallway. Having her own accommodations at the end of the hall was convenient, as it gave her privacy, yet proximity to the kitchen, where she usually started and ended each day. Only Betty's room was in the same hallway, which she found a relief. As she'd grown continually fonder of the hotelkeeper over the years, it eased her mind to know Betty could reach her easily, if needed.

Setting her tea down on a crocheted doily by her bed, Mist moved to her easel, which was already set with small canvas squares. Having established a tradition of offering a miniature painting to each guest on Christmas morning, she sat back and contemplated the blank canvases. With so many new guests this year, the squares seemed emptier than usual. Shifting in her seat, she wondered how this could be. It was as if the squares were simply air, not even canvas. If she touched a brush to one of them, would it simply pass through the other side? It was the only image that came to mind. Other than with Michael and the professor, she had no frame of reference for any of this year's guests.

Preparing her paints, she arranged the colors in a row, from the most muted to the brightest. Selectively, she applied a base color to each small canvas until a quilt of varied colors filled her easel. Perhaps the colors and personalities would draw themselves together as the guests became more familiar to her and to each other. The whimsical thought even hit her that they might simply depart with a square of color. This sudden notion tickled her such that she laughed out loud, a bold exclamation uncharacteristic for her usual calm manner. Clasping a hand over her mouth, she stepped away from the easel, regained her composure, and proceeded to put the paints away.

Once settled in bed, she pulled a down comforter up under her chin and closed her eyes. Even as she drifted off to sleep, a faint smile crept across her face. *A square of color, indeed!*

SIX

As was her habit, Mist was awake by five-thirty in the morning, in plenty of time to stretch and do deep breathing exercises to ease into what would surely be a busy day. Dressing in soft layers of cotton, she arrived in the kitchen by six to pre-heat the oven for the lemon-poppy seed muffins she planned to serve for breakfast. She then ran fresh coffee beans through the grinder, fixed a small pot of coffee in the kitchen for Betty and herself, and set up a more expansive beverage service in the front lobby. Many guests and townsfolk wouldn't stir until the café doors opened for breakfast at seven. But having coffee set out by six-thirty was important, if only so Clive could sneak in for a cup.

"Good morning." Betty's voice surprised Mist, who wasn't used to seeing her much before breakfast started.

"You're up early," Mist said. "I hope you weren't having trouble sleeping." She smiled at the hotelkeeper's morning appearance, which she found to be one of Betty's most endearing looks. Her faded rose chenille bathrobe was a good thirty years old, but so soft and comfortable that Betty wouldn't think of replacing it, much less her slippers from the same era. Above all, Mist loved the way Betty let her hair hang loose before dressing for the day. The kitchen lights always caught the silver strands in a manner Mist found enchanting.

"Not at all," Betty said as she poured a mug of coffee and took a seat at the center island. "I fell asleep early reading, so woke up early. I thought you might like extra help, between serving breakfast and greeting the remaining arrivals."

Mist placed the muffins in the oven, set a kitchen timer, and poured herself a mug of coffee, as well. "All will be fine. The rooms are ready, and breakfast will be simple today – an egg or tofu scramble with mushrooms and sun-dried tomatoes, served with fresh berries and lemon-poppy muffins. Maisie will drop by to help in case guests arrive before breakfast is over. Besides, you have the cookie exchange this afternoon. That will keep you busy enough."

Betty's face brightened. "Yes, it's my favorite event of the year. And some residents have gotten quite creative with recipes this time. I dare say we should call it an everything-sweet exchange."

Mist laughed. "It doesn't have the same ring to it, I'm afraid."

"You're right. We'll stick with 'cookie exchange,' as is the tradition." Betty took another sip of coffee and then set the mug down. "Speaking of which, I have molasses sugar cookies wrapped and ready to put out. Made them myself," she added with a look of pride.

"Yes, the delightful aroma floated throughout the hotel yesterday afternoon." Mist closed her eyes and inhaled, as if enjoying the gingery smell that very moment. "It was exquisite."

"The cookies weren't bad, either," Betty said. An impish expression crossed on her face. "Of course I had to test a few."

"As did Clive, I imagine," Mist said.

"Naturally." Betty chuckled. "He does consider himself the official taste-tester around here, after all." She stood, finished her coffee, and put the empty mug in the sink. "I'd better go make myself presentable before guests arrive." The statement brought a smile to Mist's face, knowing Betty's equal intention was to dress, pin her hair up, and dab on a bit of makeup before Clive showed up for breakfast. As it was, she'd barely left the room when Clive poked his head in the kitchen door.

"Something smells good," Clive said. He held a cup of coffee from the lobby, as Mist already knew he would.

"Lemon-poppy seed muffins," Mist said. "And not ready for testing yet, I'm afraid. Another five minutes should be about right."

"I am a patient man," Clive said. "I can manage that." He took a seat. "Anything I can help with today? The gallery doesn't open until noon."

Mist brought the kitchen's coffee pot over to Clive and topped off his cup. "I don't think so. Maisie's going to help with breakfast. A few more guests will be arriving, but their rooms are prepared. And Betty seems ready for the annual cookie exchange this afternoon. It should be a smooth day."

"A smooth day is a good day." Clive nodded his head as if pondering a profound idea.

Mist opened the oven door and checked the muffins, determining another minute of baking was needed. Moving to the refrigerator, she brought out the ingredients for the breakfast scrambles and set them alongside two large skillets on the stove. Sounds from the front hall indicated her timing was perfect. Guests were rising for the day and heading to the lobby for coffee and tea. Townsfolk wouldn't be far behind.

"Good morning," Betty said, entering the kitchen with hair and makeup properly in place for the day. Her forest green pants and sweater, coupled with a Christmas-themed vest, gave her a festive seasonal look. Clive wasted no time greeting her with a kiss, though it didn't escape his vision that Mist was taking the muffins out of the oven.

"I believe I only have half your attention, Clive," Betty teased. She patted his shoulder playfully. "I see you eyeing those muffins."

"It's not my fault that Mist is such a good cook, you know," Clive protested.

"Well, now, you have a good point there," Betty said.

Mist felt a surge of happiness watching the two senior lovebirds banter back and forth. Leaving them to continue their morning chatter, she headed to the café to check the buffet and table settings, as well as the coffee and tea in the front entry area. Olga Savinova was just tapping her way down the hallway with her cane.

"Good morning, Ms. Savinova," Mist said. "I hope you slept well. Would you care for any coffee or tea?"

"I slept very well, indeed, and please call me Olga. Tea sounds delicious."

Mist fixed a cup of tea and escorted the woman into the café, so that she wouldn't have to juggle the tea with her cane to move again. It never hurt to open the café a few minutes early. Besides, she could already hear footsteps approaching both outside and on the interior stairway. Not surprisingly, Clayton was the first to arrive, as was his habit. Maisie accompanied him, but veered off toward the kitchen as he took a seat. Mist brought out a large bowl of berries, as well as the lemon-poppy seed muffins – minus one that Clive had "tested," of course.

"What a lovely café," Luisa Rivera said as she entered. Maria followed, navigating her own wheelchair into the room, her father behind her. Seeing them enter, Mist suggested a seating not far from the doorway where three chairs surrounded a four-sided table, making it easy for Maria to take a place.

"Thank you," Mist said. "It's really a community gathering place. You'll see some of our townsfolk come join in for meals."

Michael was the next to arrive, bounding down the stairs with agility. This made Mist's heart leap with joy. After seeing him limp at times in the past while he fought off a tumor in his leg, it was apparent this was a year of remission. He exchanged warm smiles with Mist and took a seat at Clayton's table.

One by one, hotel guests and local residents arrived, sharing conversation with each other and enjoying the breakfast scrambles that Maisie brought out from the kitchen. The professor chose a seat at the same table as Olga, which precipitated an animated discussion of Russian versus English tea cultures.

Shortly before the last breakfast diners departed, Mist saw Liam Gallagher, one of several guests due to arrive, step into the lobby. If she hadn't already known he was a dancer, his lithe posture would have betrayed it. His dark hair, pale skin, and blue eyes combined with the black turtleneck sweater he wore under a winter coat to make an elegant statement. He might have well been a print model.

"Welcome," Mist said. She took his coat, hoping he would offer his name before she had to guess which of two expected male guests he might be. "I'm Mist. We're just finishing up breakfast servings. You should help yourself, if you'd like."

"Liam Gallagher," he said, reaching out to shake her hand. Mist noted a faint Irish accent as he spoke. "And I'm early. I imagine these are last night's guests. I don't want to intrude."

"Nonsense," Mist said, surprising herself with the casual response. "These are not only last night's guests, but also today's townsfolk, and now one of tonight's guests, and anyone else who may walk through that door."

"Yes," Betty said, stepping into the lobby to offer help with registration. "I'd do as she says. She can be a tough one."

Liam laughed, immediately relaxing. "I find that a little hard to believe at first impression, but I'll have to take your word for it." Setting his luggage by the staircase, he followed Mist into the cafe. Seeing a newcomer arrive, the professor waved him over, adding yet an Irish twist to the tea discussion.

After the last breakfast was served, Mist and Betty made quick work of the dishes, leaving the kitchen clean and ready for the day.

"Hectic already," Betty noted.

Mist smiled. "We have three more guests to arrive, a cookie exchange, Christmas Eve dinner, and the Christmas brunch and morning celebrations ahead of us. I have a feeling we haven't even touched the surface."

SEVEN

Heather and Keira Dawson arrived shortly after one pm, looking very much related to each other with blonde hair, slim build and angular facial features. If not for their twenty year age difference and varying heights, they might have been mistaken for twins. As it was, ten-year old Keira and Heather Dawson were clearly mother and daughter.

With Betty in the kitchen, preparing for the cookie exchange shortly to follow, Mist greeted the two arriving guests and helped them with registration and their luggage. No sooner had the Dawsons been shown to their room, Mist returned to the lobby to find the remaining guest had arrived.

Matthew Brooks wasn't elderly, but wasn't as young as Liam Gallagher. He exhibited the same regal posture that Mist had noted when Liam arrived, yet boasted a few more pounds and closely cropped salt-and-pepper hair. More outgoing initially than the younger of the two men, Matthew shook Mist's hand enthusiastically and introduced himself before she said a word.

"Welcome to The Timberton Hotel," Mist said. "You've arrived right behind two other cast members, and another arrived this morning. We're so sorry to hear of your misfortune, but delighted to have you here with us. Let us know if we can help with anything during your stay."

"Thank you," Matthew said. "I'll admit it's been a tough few days, but we're happy that you had room for us. We're looking forward to spending Christmas at your hotel."

Mist led Matthew to the counter, gave him a registration card to sign, and handed him the key to his room, explaining its upstairs location. She offered to escort him to the room, but he assured her he could find it.

"Matt! You're here!"

Mist and Matthew both turned to see Keira racing down the stairs. Her approach resembled a tomboy running to climb a tree more than a ballet dancer hurrying to meet another cast member.

"Pardon me, dear Clara," Matthew said solemnly. "But I believe that is *Herr Drosselmeyer* to you." He crossed his arms dramatically, but opened them just in time for Keira to hug him. Their affection for each other was clear.

"Is Liam here?" Keira asked, turning to Mist, wide-eyed.

"Yes, he arrived this morning." Mist marveled at Keira's enthusiasm. Knowing how many young girls aspired to the role of Clara in The Nutcracker, it couldn't have been easy *to* have the last performances cancelled, especially under such dire circumstances. "I think you'll find him in the front parlor with some of the other guests."

"The Cavalier!" Keira shouted and then blushed. "Oops, sorry, Matt," she added apologetically before running off to join the other guests.

Mist and Matthew laughed, both amused by Keira's antics.

"Is she always this cheerful? Energetic?" Mist asked. "It's charming - inspiring, really."

"She seems to be," Matthew said.

"Unless she has to do the dishes," a female voice chimed in. "In which case that lovely energy seems to disappear quickly."

Mist turned to see Keira's mother coming down the stairs. "I was never very fond of household chores myself growing up," Mist said, laughing. "So I understand."

"Good to see you, Heather," Matthew said, grasping his suitcase. "I'm off to get settled in, but will be back down to visit later." Mist reminded him to let her know if he needed anything, and then turned her attention back to Heather as he headed up the stairs.

"There is another guest here who is the same age as your daughter," Mist said.

Heather smiled. "Perfect. Keira was sad to see the other children in the show leave. She'll be glad to know she's not stuck with a bunch of boring adults for the holidays."

Betty entered in time to hear the comment on her way to look out the front window. "I'm not sure you'll find any of the adults here boring," she laughed. "But I know children like to be around others their own age."

The sound of pre-teen giggles floated out from the front parlor. Mist and Heather exchanged knowing looks. "It sounds like the two have already hit it off," Heather said.

"It does, indeed," Mist said, stepping back as the front door opened, and two women from the church ladies' guild entered, large platters of baked goods in hand.

"Cookie exchange," Mist explained.

"A yearly tradition," Betty added as she ushered the women through to the café.

"Let's go see where that youthful laughter came from," Mist suggested. She and Heather moved to the front parlor, where they found most of the hotel guests gathered in various groupings. Luisa and Rafael stood by the Christmas tree, admiring the hotel's old-fashioned ornaments. Michael, Olga and the professor sat near the fireplace, the two men in discussion, Olga listening intently. Keira and Maria sat side by side, Keira on a small stool, Maria in her wheelchair. The giggles turned out to be a result of animated storytelling on the part of Liam, who had both girls under his spell.

Mist introduced Heather to Keira's parents, knowing that having the children in common would provide for easy conversation. She passed by Michael, Olga and the professor, amused to find the tea discussion had resumed. Maria waved her over to hear a portion of Liam's current tale – something about an iridescent dragon who gave children rides around the moon in exchange for red licorice. Pleased to see the guests enjoying each other's company, she turned on some light Christmas music and excused herself to see if Betty needed any assistance.

In the short time Mist had spent with guests in the front parlor, a dozen additional townsfolk had shown up for the cookie exchange. Sally, who owned Second Hand Sally's, the local thrift shop, had made peanut butter fudge that closely rivaled the white Christmas fudge that Marge brought from her own candy store. Millie had shown up with a variety of date treats, including date nut bars, date balls, and a powdered date concoction with a half walnut hidden inside. Glenda, from the Curl 'N Cue Salon, whose kitchen was being remodeled, proved that sweets could be just as delicious without the luxury of a working oven. Her no-bake healthy apple bites and peanut butter oatmeal cookies were both hits.

"Can you believe the variety this year?" Betty sidled over near Mist and offering her some mocha candied nuts. "Clayton's mother brought peanut brittle that cooks in a microwave. Imagine that! And I don't know how Maisie managed to pull off Minty Chocolate Macarons with little Clay Jr. crawling around, but she did."

"I may have gained five pounds just walking into this room," Mist said, eyeing a basket of assorted cookies on its way in.

"Marge brought wire baskets lined with parchment paper for everyone to fill," Betty said. "She's been using those for gift baskets this year. I've seen a few of them displayed in her store. It's nice she had enough to share with everyone here today."

"Christmas brings generosity out in people," Mist said. Seeing Betty's non-committal look, she whispered, "not always, I know, but often enough that we can believe in little miracles."

"You simply must try this," Maisie said, one arm securing Clay Jr. on her hip, the other balancing a chocolate-toffee concoction. "Millie's niece Kim brought it over. It's called Christmas Crack."

Betty and Mist both leaned forward to inspect the goods. "Looks like it would go well with a cup of tea later," Mist said. "Maybe you could hide a couple pieces in the kitchen?"

"And hide them well, where Clive won't find them" Betty added, laughing. "He'll be looking for sure."

"Will do," Maisie said. She winked, hoisted Clay Jr. higher on her hip, and headed for the kitchen.

Betty turned to Mist. "Why don't you put together a selection for the guests to enjoy in the front parlor? We have plenty this year, more than enough. I just won't make a basket myself. We always have the glazed cinnamon nuts, plus I made extra molasses sugar cookies."

Not one to turn down a suggestion that would please the guests, Mist selected a variety of everything and returned to the front parlor, where Matthew had now joined the group. The two girls were now huddled together, exchanging what Mist assumed to be secrets by the whispering and cupped hands. Liam had joined Olga, who had moved to a table in the back of the room. The two were engaged in a discussion that seemed serious, yet light, based on the smiles accompanying their conversation. Luisa and Rafael now sat near the fire, quietly enjoying the music. Michael and Nigel – Mist could still not bring herself to call him anything but "the professor" – had gone for a walk down to Clive's gallery. Everyone appeared content, especially when the basket of sweets passed around the room.

Mist took a position near the tree, observing the scene. The colored canvas squares in her room were already taking on vague forms, though not yet defined clearly. Yet her mind swayed toward the evening meal she would prepare after the cookie exchange participants departed, baskets brimming with treats for their families. Juggling the energy of a full hotel required balance. For Mist, that meant some time alone to recharge. With artwork, cooking, and continued hospitality in mind, she retired to her room.

EIGHT

"Did you see the girls outside?" Betty asked. "I'm glad it's not a cold winter this year. We do have some snow, but it's comfortable with the sun out. They're both wearing coats, anyway. Luisa made sure before helping Maria out and leaving the two together. You should look. It's wonderful the way they've become friends so quickly."

Mist set aside the rosemary and garlic she was using to prepare roasted root vegetables and peeked out the window. She smiled. "I remember that."

"Remember what?" Betty moved to stand by Mist and popped a powdered walnut date in her mouth. "These are very good, by the way."

"Those arm positions that Keira is showing Maria," Mist said. "I took ballet lessons when I was young. I recognize the progression: first, second, third, fourth, and high fifth."

"And then she places her arms in a circle in her lap," Betty observed.

"That would be a low fifth, or as close as it's possible for Maria, since she can't stand."

Betty sighed. "It's a shame she isn't able to dance. I'll bet those two would be dancing through the snow together."

"She *is* dancing," Mist said. "Any one of us can dance with our arms, or even with our imaginations."

"Anyone?" Betty murmured. She held her arms in a circle over the sink. "I'm not sure this would apply to Clive," she snickered.

Mist laughed. "You may have a point there, but I still believe he could. I bet he could mimic that position just by reaching around you for a hug."

"I may have to test that theory," Betty said. A giggle escaped her lips that almost matched those of the girls earlier in the afternoon. Mist noted that the girls' arm movements had stopped and they were now engaged in what looked like a serious discussion.

The kitchen door opened, and Michael stuck his head in. "Can I help with anything?"

"You know you're a guest," Mist pointed out, though grinning. "You don't need to help with anything."

"But I'm a special guest," Michael quipped, stepping into the kitchen.

"How are your ballet arms?" Betty asked, resulting in a baffled look on Michael's face. "You could practice over the sink. Or ..." She took her coat off a hook by the back door and started to put it on. Michael crossed the kitchen and helped her. "I think I'll go visit Clive for a bit." She grinned and slipped out the door.

"What was that about?" Michael asked, looking more confused than ever.

"Come over to the sink. I'll show you." Mist moved to the window that looked out into the yard, seeing that the girls had resumed the arm movements. Michael, dubious, followed.

"I see what you're talking about now," Michael said, watching the girls. "I had a chance to chat with Luisa in the front room earlier. She said Maria always dreamed of becoming a ballerina. She had just started lessons before the accident that cost her the use of her legs. She's thrilled to meet Keira."

"Sometimes we can live our dreams through others," Mist said. "It's one of life's many miracles." She looked out the window again, noting Olga had joined the girls. Keira raised her arms to first position, and Olga reached out and touched one of Keira's wrists while tapping her cane in the snow. Both girls appeared to be completely entranced.

Michael turned to Mist. "Now what was Betty saying about practicing over the sink?"

Mist lifted her arms, forming a circle without her fingers touching. "You try it."

"Like this?" Michael copied Mist's movement, though far less gracefully.

"Close enough," Mist said, smiling. She moved back to the tray of vegetables and placed several sprigs of rosemary around the assortment of beets, carrots and potatoes.

"But why was she …" Michael followed Mist, but glanced toward the back door, as if Betty were still there. "I dare say she was giggling when she left."

"Oh, that." Mist sprinkled freshly chopped garlic around the rosemary. "I told her Clive could mimic a ballet arm position by hugging her." She purposely left out the fact that Betty's plump figure would help his arms form a similar circle to that which the girls were practicing.

Predictably, Michael walked around and stood behind Mist, circling his arms around her waist. "Like this?"

"Mist laughed. "No, your arms need to be looser, so your fingers don't touch."

"Really? I disagree," Michael said. "I think they need to be tighter, so that the hands cross over each other."

Mist could hear the smile in his voice as he crossed his arms, one over the other, and brought her closer to him. She set the garlic down and turned around to face him, still wrapped in his embrace. "I'm glad you took the teaching job up in Missoula. It will be nice to have you closer to Timberton."

"I had hoped to get in for the spring semester," Michael admitted. "But the current spot in the literature department didn't open up until fall. It's a better fit for my background than the few earlier openings. Philosophy, for example. That might suit you better. Though I dare say some of your philosophical twists might not fit in with the usual curriculum."

"Then the students would have to look at everything with an open mind," Mist said. "That is always a good thing." She coyly extricated herself from Michael's arms, covered the tray of vegetables, and set them aside to bake at the appropriate time.

A knock on the kitchen door preceded another head popping in from behind the door.

"Is this the afternoon meeting place?" Matthew asked. His cheerful expression and missing body reminded Mist of a cartoon character peeking around a tree. "Front parlor in the evening, and kitchen in the afternoon?"

"It appears to be today," Mist said. "And why not?" She waved Matthew in and offered him a seat at the center island. "I can offer you coffee or tea, but no dinner previews."

"Clive gets to do all the taste-testing around here," Michael pointed out.

"Only because he's developed sneaky skills over the last few years," Mist added.

Matthew accepted a mug of coffee and looked around. "So this is where the magic happens. I've heard about your legendary cooking, Mist."

"Magic happens everywhere," Mist said. "A kitchen, a hotel, a park, a stage …" She left the sentence open-ended, knowing Matthew would pick up on it.

"True," Matthew said. "There's something special about what occurs on stage, and between the stage and the audience. We never know quite what it will be from one show to the next, but there's definitely something magical there. Speaking of which, I was hoping that Betty might be here." He glanced around and then looked back at Mist. "But I think I could ask you." We never know quite what it will be from one show to the next, but there's definitely something magical there. Speaking of which, I was hoping that Betty might be here." He glanced around and then looked back at Mist. "But I think I could ask you."

"Well, you have me quite curious now," Mist said. "So I hope you'll go ahead. Maybe there's something we could do to make your stay more comfortable?"

Matthew shook his head. "Oh, golly, no. I can't imagine being more comfortable than I am here. But I was talking with Liam and we thought your other guests might enjoy a small holiday presentation after your Christmas Eve dinner tomorrow night."

"That sounds intriguing," Mist said. "We usually gather in the front parlor after the meal, but not with anything in particular planned - just listening to Christmas music, sometimes singing, always enjoying each other's company. What did you have in mind?"

"We thought we might give a very miniature version of The Nutcracker. Obviously the space is tiny compared to a stage, and most of our cast members are missing, but we could do a simple fifteen-to-twenty minute version, almost like a skit."

"A wonderful idea!" Michael exclaimed, and then looked at Mist, who was staring at him with amusement. "Of course," Michael added quickly, "This would be up to Betty and Mist."

"It's only a suggestion," Matthew continued. "And it would involve moving furniture, which might be something you'd prefer not to do. But Keira would be delighted to show off a bit of her Clara role, and Liam and I could act out a few parts." He took a sip of coffee. "Just something to think about."

Mist placed both hands on the counter and closed her eyes, envisioning the possibility. A space could easily be cleared, still leaving enough chairs around the room for an audience. She would run it by Betty, but was sure her response would be the same.

"That would be amazing," Mist said after she opened her eyes. "It would make for lovely Christmas Eve entertainment. Also nice for Keira after having the shows cancelled. I'll make sure, but I'm certain Betty will like the idea."

"What idea will I like?" Conveniently, Betty stepped in through the kitchen's side door in time to hear the last sentence. She took off her coat and hat, and then joined the others.

"Matthew has proposed a short Nutcracker presentation after dinner tomorrow night," Mist said. She watched Betty for her reaction, but already knew what it would be.

"Oh, my! What a treat that would be!" Betty's face lit up. "But how …"

"It could work quite easily," Mist said. "We'll rearrange the furniture a bit, and I might be able to pull together some type of costumes."

"No need," Matthew said. "We had just enough time to pull personal belongings and some costumes and props from the theatre when we left. So we have a few things with us.

"I say it's a wonderful plan," Betty said.

"I agree," Mist said. "This will be such fun for the other guests, as well as a few townsfolk who might linger after dinner."

Matthew nodded. "Great. I'll talk to Liam and we'll work out a plan."

"Clive and Clayton could help with set-up, if needed," Betty said She glanced at Michael. "And it appears we have a guest who might help, too."

"Gladly," Michael said.

"It's settled, then," Betty said. "It will be a special Christmas Eve indeed."

Mist smiled. "They are all special. And this will be no exception."

NINE

Mist sauntered through the café, checking on guests. The enthusiastic conversations at various tables pleased her. It was a smaller crowd than usual, in spite of the high hotel occupancy. Not surprisingly, many townsfolk had chosen to dine at home, saving the Moonglow Café for the now legendary Christmas Eve meal the following night.

Most of the hotel guests had chosen to sit together at the largest table, their group sounding particularly lively. It seemed the idea of a Nutcracker mini-performance had kicked the already joyful holiday spirit up an extra notch.

"This zucchini strata is splendid," Nigel said as Mist passed by. "What is this great combination of cheeses?"

"Provolone, white cheddar, feta and parmesan," Mist said. "But it would not taste the same without garlic and parsley, to give credit where credit is due."

"Well, it's truly fit for the mouse king!" The professor took another bite and rephrased. "Or perhaps I should say 'der mausekonig.'"

"Dare … mouse …cone … ick?" Maria, seated at the same table, tried to copy the professor's pronunciation. Keira, seated beside her, attempted to do the same with equal difficulty.

"Close, my dear children," Nigel said. "'Nussknacker und Mausekonig' is German for 'The Nutcracker and the Mouse King.' It was the original name of the story written by E.T.A. Hoffman that is now The Nutcracker."

Keira and Maria looked at each other, and then back at the professor, confused. "But I thought it was Russian," Keira said. "The music is."

"Music is a language of its own," Mist said.

"I knew she was going to say that," Clive said, seated at a table close enough to overhear. Betty, sitting next to Clive, tapped him on the arm playfully and told him to hush, although she was smiling as she did so. Clive's teasing of Mist's view of life had become almost as predictable as Mist's statements themselves.

"Yes," Nigel said. "You are partially correct, Keira. The music was written by the Russian composer, Pyotr Ilyich Tchaikovsky."

Maria spoke up in defense of her new friend. "Why is she only partially correct, Professor, if Tchaikovsky was Russian?"

"Because the original story was German," Keira said, understanding.

This time Olga spoke up. "I can make that more complicated, if you'd like."

Nigel smiled. "I would be chuffed to hear it from you, Ms. Savinova." Both girls snickered at the word "chuffed," being unfamiliar with British English.

"E.T.A. Hoffman's story was not actually the one Tchaikovsky based his story on," Olga said. "That version was French. It was called 'Histoire d'un Casse Noisette' and was written by Alexandre Dumas."

"An exceptional French author," Michael said. "If you girls end up studying French literature later in your schooling, you'll undoubtedly read some of his work."

"So they really all wrote the story together," Maria said, trying to put the information together. German, French, Russian."

"In a way," Nigel said. "But they all lived at different times. Hoffman wrote his story in the early 1816, and Dumas wrote his in 1844, quite a while after Hoffman passed away. So, although it was essentially the same story, they didn't work together on it. Rather, Dumas wrote his own version."

"And then Tchaikovsky added the music," Keira said.

"Yes," Liam said. "And fabulous music, at that."

"Absolutely," Matthew agreed. "I never tire of it."

"The music was not added until 1892," Olga said, "which is when Marius Petipa and Lev Ivanov added choreography, and it premiered in St. Petersburg at the Mariinsky Theatre." Both girls looked at Olga, as did several other guests. Noting their attention, Olga added simply, "I'm from St. Petersburg originally. I know some of the history." Satisfied with the explanation, the general conversation resumed.

"Imagine seeing it for the very first time!" Maria exclaimed.

"Yes!" Keira said. "The audience must have been so excited!"

"I'm afraid not," Olga said. "It was not well-received. The reviews were very mixed."

"But it's so famous!" Maria said.

"It is now," Matthew pointed out. "But nothing is famous the first time. It is simply new."

"Many times art isn't recognized until years after it is created," Liam said "It can be decades or even centuries."

"That applies to many forms of art," Michael added. "Not just dance, but writing, music, painting, and more."

Keira and Maria both fell silent. After a moment, Keira picked up her fork and stabbed a piece of zucchini. "That hardly seems fair," she said. "Then artists don't get to know if they create something famous."

Nigel nodded. "Indeed. But fair or not, that is how it is sometimes."

"That means the first girl who played Clara didn't know how special it was," Maria said, as if that idea alone topped everything.

"Actually, the first Clara wasn't named Clara," Olga said, practically causing both girls to drop their forks. "The young girl in the original German story was named Marie, which is the name George Balanchine used for his ballet later on."

"I've heard of him," Keira said nonchalantly.

"I should hope so," Olga said, fighting back a smile. "And some Russian productions called the character "Masha."

"Weird." Both girls responded together.

"However," Olga said, directing her comment to Maria. "Would you like to know what the Bolshoi Ballet called that part?" Getting an affirmative nod, she added, "Maria."

"Really?" Maria said. "Well, I used to dream of being Clara. I guess I have been all along." Pleased with that thought, she turned to Keira. "And now I get to watch you be me."

"Want to watch us rehearse tomorrow?" Keira asked. "I mean, if that's okay."

Maria turned to her mother. "Mom?"

Luisa and Rafael exchanged looks. Rafael nodded. "I don't see why not," Luisa said.

"What's for dessert?" Clive asked suddenly, as if food had been the subject of discussion all along.

Betty stood up, laughing. "He's incorrigible," she said. "But I bet Mist and I can dig something up." She picked up several finished dinner dishes and headed for the kitchen.

"It's possible," Mist said. Excusing herself, she accompanied Betty.

"Possible means probable," Clive said.

Minutes later, Mist and Betty reappeared with small glass bowls of mixed strawberries and apple slices accompanied by caramel and chocolate dipping sauces.

"Mix and match as you please," Mist said. "You're welcome to take them in by the fireplace if you'd like. I'll have espresso, decaf, and peppermint tea set out in a few minutes." She smiled at Maria, whose face lit up at the mention of peppermint tea, and then turned back to the group. "You may want to enjoy the front parlor for this evening, as it will be off-limits most of the day tomorrow."

Some guests nodded with understanding, others simply to be polite.

"Meanwhile," Betty said, "if some of you are wondering where to go while waiting for Christmas Eve dinner tomorrow afternoon, you're welcome to head to Clive's place. He'll be having a reception at his gallery."

"I will?" Clive said, almost choking on a chocolate-covered strawberry. Catching the mischievous grins on both Betty and Mist's faces, he swallowed and smiled. "I mean, yes, I will."

TEN

Heather and Luisa sat on the sofa near the fireplace, their desserts balanced on their laps. Matthew had enlisted Rafael's help in bringing in firewood while Mist added the last available log inside to the fire.

"It's wonderful the way the girls have formed such a close friendship," Heather said. She indicated a far corner of the room, where Keira and Maria sat huddled together. Olga sat on a chair beside the girls, listening and occasionally inserting comments into their discussion.

"Yes, I'm pleased," Luisa said. "Maria does not always make friends easily. Many of the other girls in her class are involved with soccer or other physical activities that she can't do."

"That must be difficult for her - and for you," Heather said.

"It is at times," Luisa admitted. "But she has such a positive attitude. She doesn't let it get her down. And she does have other interests. She loves to read, for example. She's insatiable when it comes to books."

"Keira, too," Heather said. "If she's not dancing, she's reading. Sometimes she ever tries to read *while* dancing."

"I can barely walk and talk at the same time," Matthew said as he and Rafael brought firewood in from outside. He handed one log to Mist, which she added to the fire. "It's a good thing I went into dance instead of musical theatre."

"A good thing for all of us," Liam added, drawing a laugh from the crowd.

Satisfied the second log was properly settled in the fireplace, Mist turned toward the others. "We all have strengths and weaknesses," Mist said.

Michael, who had been reading in his favorite chair, set his book down. "I believe that is coming from someone who has no weaknesses," he said.

Mist, in a gesture very unusual for her, placed her hands on her hips. "That most certainly is not true."

"Then you keep them well hidden," Heather said, ready to side with Michael. Luisa and Matthew nodded, as well.

"That's because you've never seen me try to hit a softball, or solve a chemistry problem, or ride a horse, or dozens of other things I've attempted unsuccessfully," Mist said. Her voice softened. "I'm no different than anyone else."

"I'm not sure I'd go that far," Michael said. "But I do see your point. I love to teach, for example. However, you wouldn't want me on your basketball team, and if a button fell off my shirt, I'd be looking for help to sew it back on." He winked at Mist.

"I have no problem with sewing," Mist said, smiling, "as long as I'm asked nicely." She had barely uttered the words when Betty entered.

"Glenda just dropped this off for you," Betty said, handing Mist a bag with the thrift shop logo on it. "She said you'd know what it was for."

"Yes," Mist said. "I spoke with her earlier today." She glanced inside the bag, smiled, and looked back up at the guests. "Please excuse me while I attend to some preparations for tomorrow."

Leaving the others to enjoy the fire, Mist passed through the kitchen and down the back hall to her room. There, on her doorknob, she found a second bag she'd been expecting, just as Keira said it would be. She entered her room, closed the door quietly, and removed the contents from both bags.

The layers of white satin and toile that tumbled from Keira's bag were as beautiful as she had imagined. Her task, as Keira had described it, was to "make it sort of pink." The additional direction, a little trickier, was that it would need to stay white in the end, after its temporary pink livelihood ended. The item from the thrift shop would only take a few minutes to fix up.

Being a collector of knick knacks served Mist well for this particular challenge, especially her habit of picking up fabric remnants at the thrift shop. Heading down the hallway again, she rummaged through her closet of treasured items. She found a length of pink chiffon, a bag of lavender organza rosebuds, and a loose assortment of satin ribbons. Gathering it all together, she retreated to her room and set to work. Two hours later, she stood back and examined the result of her efforts, quite sure that Keira would be pleased. Maria, too, would likely be delighted.

Mist returned to the front parlor, now empty other than Michael, who still sat by the fire, reading, as she knew he would be. This had always been his habit, long before Mist arrived in Timberton and established the café that was now housed in the hotel. And she understood it completely. The idea of having a few days to simply sit by a fire for hours and read sounded like a perfect vacation.

"And she appears again," Michael said, looking up from his book.

"I promised Keira a favor earlier," Mist said. "A couple favors, actually."

Michael nodded. "Something to do with the secrets the two girls seem to be constantly whispering to each other?"

"Perhaps," Mist said, purposely making her voice sound mysterious.

"I suspect you have other tasks to attend to," Michael said. "Please don't feel you need to stay and visit. You have quite a full house this year."

"I only have one important task at the moment," Mist said, sitting down on the sofa.

"And what would that be?" Michael smiled, suspecting the answer already.

"To sit here and enjoy your company, perhaps with some tea." She started to rise, but Michael stood and gently encouraged her to sit back down.

"I'll get the tea," Michael said. "It just so happens that this hotel has tea and coffee service all set up in the lobby. Did you know that?"

"I've heard a rumor to that effect," Mist said. She tilted her head to one side, then to the other, just to add a whimsical touch to her reply.

"Betty even refilled the hot water just a short while ago," Michael added. "You just rest."

Mist started to protest, but Michael's determined expression stopped her. Giving in, she relaxed against the back of the sofa. A few minutes later, Michael set a cup of tea on the side table next to the sofa, where Mist could reach it. Sitting beside her, he placed his arm around her shoulders and eased her head over to rest against him. She closed her eyes, letting herself be lulled by the warmth of the fire on one side and the beating of Michael's heart on the other.

"There is an art exhibit at the university next month," Michael said as he rubbed her arm affectionately. "I'm hoping you might come up to see it."

"That sounds delightful," Mist said sleepily. "I'd love to."

"February might be a nice time for a visit, too," Michael said.

"I agree," Mist murmured.

"And March …"

"Mmm …"

After that, only the crackling of the fire remained, mixed with a very faint snoring, which, in view of it being Mist, was really just a soft purr.

ELEVEN

"It's fortunate we don't serve breakfast or lunch on Christmas Eve," Betty said. "Clayton and his fire crew are making quite the ruckus out there in the front parlor."

Mist laughed. "We have too much to do just to get ready for dinner. Besides, they're having fun, I can tell."

"What gave it away?" Betty asked. "The 'ninety-nine bottles of eggnog on the wall' song they've improvised?"

"That and the 'top secret - do not enter' sign they have on the door," Mist said.

"It looks like a boys' clubhouse." Betty shook her head.

"All the more charming for that," Mist said as she arranged fresh cut vegetables, olives, marinated mushrooms, and petite gherkins on a large platter. "It was kind of Clayton to offer to set up for the presentation tonight."

"I had no idea he'd done lighting work for his college theatre productions," Betty said. "He was excited about helping, said it brought back some good memories. Plus he has all those tools and ladders and whatnot from the fire station."

"Yes, convenient to have all that on hand," Mist said. She placed a china sleigh filled with toothpicks in the center of the platter and covered it. "There," she said. "All ready for the reception at Clive's place later this afternoon."

"*That* was a clever last-minute way to get everyone out of the hotel this afternoon," Betty said. "And worth it just to see the shock on Clive's face!"

"A logical and pleasant solution," Mist said. "With Clayton rearranging furniture and working on lighting in the front parlor, and the two of us preparing the café for tonight's dinner, the guests needed a comfortable place to spend the afternoon."

"It's also good for Clive," Betty said. "He'll get to show off his gallery."

"Yes," Mist said. "He's excited about it. I dare say he thinks it's like having his own cookie exchange."

"Not a bad idea," Betty said. "Maybe he should do this every year, a Christmas Eve gallery reception."

"That would be one way to keep him out of the kitchen, trying to steal bites of food before dinner is ready," Mist said. "Then again, it wouldn't be quite the same without him sneaking in."

"True, and I bet he'd find ways to do it, anyway," Betty said.

Mist laughed. "I'm sure he would." She set the appetizer tray aside, knowing Maisie would pick it up later and take it over to Clive's place.

"What next?" Betty asked.

"How about helping me with the table and buffet decorations for tonight? I could use an extra pair of hands."

"And here I thought you were going for a simple "air" theme," Betty joked, remembering Mist's decision to remove the candy-filled mason jars before.

"Only temporarily." Mist disappeared through the door to the back hallway and reappeared with a large carton. Betty followed her into the café and watched as Mist pulled the first jar.

"Well, look at that!" Betty exclaimed. The formerly plain glass jar now boasted glitter that sparkled under the café lights, as well as a whimsical wire-rimmed bow on top, additional pieces of candy decorating the folds of ribbon.

Mist pulled more jars out and arranged them on one table, spreading the greenery from Maisie's Daisie's around the fanciful glass decorations "Yes, I think this will work." She removed others from the carton and offered one to Betty. "We just need to add more to the other tables, plus several on the buffet."

As the two women decorated the tables and buffet, voices filtered in from the lobby, and Keira, Maria, and Olga soon appeared in the café doorway.

"We're going to the library," Keira announced. She wore a warm jacket, as did the others. Maria had an additional shawl covering her lap and legs.

"Yes," Maria said, beaming. "Mother said I could go on my own as long as I have an adult with me. And Ms. Savinova is an adult."

Olga nodded and tapped her cane on the floor. "Yes, I believe I am."

"The library?" Betty said, eyebrows raised. "I don't think it's open today, girls. But we have plenty of books in the front parlor bookshelves."

"Although that room isn't available right now," Mist pointed out.

"Don't worry," Olga said. "The library visit is already arranged. I ran into your town librarian at the candy store earlier and she offered us a private tour."

"How nice of her!" Betty exclaimed. "It's a lovely library. It's not large, but it has a good selection of books, plus a new community room for town meetings and local events. There's artwork by local schoolchildren on display, too. You'll enjoy it."

"I'm sure we will," Keira said. She and Maria exchanged glances, giggling.

"I'm going that way, too," Liam said as he bounded down the stairs. "Let me help." He grasped Maria's wheelchair handles and cautiously escorted the group out the door.

"Well, what do you know," Betty said after the front door closed. "The guests are finding all kinds of ways to stay busy this afternoon."

"Yes, they are," Mist said as she interspersed votive candles with the decorations. Betty watched Mist's placement of the candles and arranged other tables in similar fashion. Once the decorated candy jars, ribbons, greenery, and candles graced both tables and buffet, Betty and Mist moved to the kitchen.

"What can I do to help?" Betty said. She poured a mug of coffee, sat down at the center island, and waited for instructions.

"Does stuffing squash sound exciting?" Mist watched with amusement as Betty pondered the question. "I'm kidding, Betty. Just keeping me company is helping." She pulled a large bowl of mushroom, pecan, cranberry and farro stuffing out of the refrigerator, along with two large trays of sweet dumpling squash, already cut in half and partially roasted.

"I don't know how you do it, Mist," Betty said. "When did you prepare all that?"

Mist smiled. "There's a reason we don't serve breakfast on Christmas Eve, remember? The squash baked while I set up coffee, tea, croissants, and juice in the lobby. The stuffing took very little time to sauté. Now we'll stuff each squash half and put them in the oven about thirty minutes before the roasted tarragon lamb is done."

"Salad? Bread? Dessert? Do tell," Betty said.

"Very simple this year," Mist said. "We'll have mixed greens with toasted almonds and champagne vinaigrette dressing, asiago-olive dinner rolls, and vanilla bean gelato, with or without a dash of peppermint schnapps on top."

"Ah," Betty said. "Now I know what's under the towels on the counter."

"Yes," Mist teased. "It's the gelato. I set it out so the yeast could rise."

"Well, on that silly note, I'm off to help Clive spruce up his gallery," Betty said. She pulled a bucket from under the kitchen sink and dropped a few supplies inside. "I have a feeling his idea of cleaning is a quick sweep with the broom."

"He'll need to clear one of his display tables to make room for the relish plate, hot cider carafes, and Christmas punch," Mist said. "Speaking of which, take these with you." She placed several oranges in a cloth bag and added a package of fresh cranberries from the refrigerator. "To float on top of the punch," she added, anticipating Betty's question.

"What will the punch go in?" Betty asked. "I suspect you're using our large crystal bowl for the salad tonight."

"Maisie's taking one over. Clayton's parents gave them a beautiful punch bowl as a wedding present." Mist handed Betty the bag of fruit, a mischievous look following. "And Pop's Parlor is donating a bit of Bacardi for those who wish to spice things up."

Betty laughed. "Timberton will be a festive town tonight, no doubt! Between Clive's gallery reception, your Christmas Eve dinner, and the sweet performance Keira, Matthew and Liam have planned, there'll be no lack of holiday spirit."

Mist watched as Betty headed out the door, fruit bag in one hand, bucket of cleaning supplies in the other. *Yes,* she mused, *enough holiday spirit to fill the hotel, the town, the guests' hearts, and a little extra to float out into the universe beyond.*

TWELVE

Maisie swept into the kitchen, Clay Jr. in her arms. "You really should go down to the gallery for a few minutes. It's such a joyous gathering."

Mist looked at Maisie as if she'd lost her mind. "You do realize I have *just a few* people coming to dinner an hour and a half from now?"

"No more than thirty," Maisie said, and then paused as Mist raised her eyebrows. "Okay, maybe forty or fifty," she admitted. "But, knowing you, you've been ready for a week."

Mist pointed across the kitchen, her arm as graceful as a sugar-plum fairy. "You see those large ovens that Clive installed for us a few years ago? I have three bone-in lamb roasts in there, as well as a seven-rib standing roast for those who prefer beef."

Maisie crossed the kitchen and looked through the glass doors to the ovens, keeping Clay Jr. safely off to the side. "One shelf is empty," she said.

"That's for the portobello mushroom wellington, for those who don't eat meat at all," Mist said. "It goes in the oven later, along with the stuffed squash and rolls."

"And your salad?" Maisie quipped.

Mist sighed, knowing where Maisie was heading with her line of questioning. "Prepared, in the refrigerator downstairs."

"I thought so." Maisie walked to the coat rack by the back door and removed a wool cape that Mist was known to wear on cold evenings. "The café is set. I saw the tables when I came in. And I will watch the roasts, in case they decide to hop around the kitchen or something while you're away. Clive's place is just a block away. Go for ten minutes."

Giving in, Mist took the cape, threw it over her shoulders, and grabbed a scarf and mittens from a shelf. In truth, she was curious to see how things were going at the gallery, and she had no justified argument against Maisie's valid points. The roasts would cook themselves, the café only needed candles lit just before guests arrived, and the front parlor was set for the after-dinner performance. In addition, she'd dressed early for the evening, donning a forest green velvet dress, ivory vest, and vintage rhinestone earrings. Bundled up, she thanked Maisie and headed out.

Mist could hear the cheerful camaraderie halfway to Clive's place. A light snow had begun falling, enough to give the gallery a snow globe appearance from outside. Windows outlined with twinkling lights framed silhouettes of guests inside, cups of punch or mugs of cider in their hands. Christmas music mixed with happy voices as she approached the doorway. She paused and smiled before opening the door. Maisie had been right. Even if she didn't step inside, it would have been worth the walk just to observe the scene from outside.

"You're here!" Keira crossed the gallery quickly and took Mist's hand, pulling her over by Maria's wheelchair. "We're so excited!" Keira said.

Maria nodded her head enthusiastically, agreeing with her new friend. "I can hardly wait to see Keira dance!" Mist smiled as both girls covered their mouths, an unsuccessful attempt to hide a new batch of giggles.

Luisa and Rafael stood nearby, each holding a cup of punch. Luisa leaned toward Mist and whispered, "I haven't seen Maria this excited in years."

"I'm glad," Mist said. "Christmas does have a way of warming the heart."

"It's wonderful to see her so happy," Rafael added, his face exhibiting fatherly pride.

Mist felt her cape being lifted off her shoulders. Turning, she was not surprised to see Michael by her side. She placed her hand lightly on his arm to stop him from moving away. "I can only stay a few minutes," she said. Understanding, Michael draped the cape over his arm, rather than take it to the coat rack near the gallery door.

"You look beautiful," Michael whispered. His lips brushed against her skin just below one ear, causing a rhinestone earring to sway and sparkle under the gallery lights.

"And you look quite dapper yourself, Mr. Blanton," Mist said, admiring the way his cashmere sweater brought out the soft green in his eyes. "As do you, Professor," Mist said as Nigel joined them. The professor's argyle vest and bow tie combined with his wire-rimmed glasses to create a statement of intellectual persuasion.

"A splendid reception," Nigel said. "I don't believe I've come down to Clive's gallery on other visits. I must make a point of visiting from now on. Your miniature paintings are delightful, for one thing. And Clive's jewelry is magnificent."

Mist thanked Nigel for his kind words, agreeing with his assessment of the jewelry. The designs Clive came up with to showcase the area's Yogo Sapphires were elegant and unique.

"I wonder what ornament he's created for Betty this year," Michael said, looking at Mist to see if she knew the answer.

"I have no idea," Mist said. "He doesn't tell anyone until he pulls it from behind the tree to present to her. That's his tradition." She reconsidered her words. "*Their* tradition is more accurate," she rephrased.

Hearty laughter caught Mist's attention, and she looked across the room to see Matthew, Liam and Clayton together near the refreshment table. Olga sat nearby, sporting an amused but demure look as she listened to whatever the three men were discussing.

"I'm pleased to see quite a few townsfolk here, especially considering this was a last-minute plan." Mist glanced around the room, spotting at least a dozen locals gathered in groups. "But," she said, turning to Michael. "I do have to get back to the hotel. Unless that relish tray on the refreshment table will satisfy everyone's appetites for the evening."

"No chance of that!" Clive said, stepping into the conversation. He wore a headband with reindeer antlers, a bright red shirt, and a bolo tie. Betty stood beside him, dressed almost identically. Instead of a bolo tie, she wore a brooch shaped like a Christmas stocking. The pair looked like they'd stepped straight out of a holiday movie.

"You heard the man," Mist said to Michael, reaching for her cape. "I'm under direct orders from Clive to make sure no one goes hungry tonight."

"Let me escort you back to the hotel," Michael offered as he helped place Mist's cape around her shoulders.

"She's going to say no," Betty said. She and Mist exchanged smiles. Betty had simply offered the answer she was about to give, anyway.

"Now that I think about it," Michael said, "we never see you right before dinner on Christmas Eve, do we?" He tilted his head to the side and regarded Mist with curiosity, as if realizing another mysterious facet of her personality.

"I don't believe you do," Mist said. She smiled as she slipped her gloves back on. Without another word, she left the gallery and headed back to the hotel.

THIRTEEN

Mist moved from table to table in the café, lighting candles and checking place settings. Maisie had left temporarily when Mist returned to the hotel, but would return to help serve dinner. Betty had stayed at the gallery to co-host the gathering with Clive. Those close to Mist knew she had a tradition of standing alone in the café before opening the doors for the Christmas Eve meal. The quiet moments before the festive activity allowed Mist to breathe in the spirit of the evening. Without sound, without music, without so much as a whisper to break the spell, the silence moved her in a way she couldn't put into words if she tried. It was a kind of magic that she only understood by the way it spoke to her soul. Surrounded by the candlelight, the elegant decorations, and the anticipation of the shared joy to come, peace descended upon her like the soft snow falling outside.

The sound of approaching footsteps broke the spell gently. Mist smiled, charmed at the thought of the approaching guests. With the front parlor off-limits this year for those waiting to dine, something new had been created: a wintery parade along Timberton's main street as the dinner guests approached.

Hearing feet shuffling on the front porch, followed by voices flowing into the hotel's front lobby, Mist opened the café doors and gestured for those arriving to enter. As the café filled with cheerful laughter, Mist retreated to the kitchen. With help from Betty and Maisie, the procession of culinary delights began, platter after platter filling the buffet until it nearly overflowed with mouth-watering goodness.

A sudden shyness passed over the crowd, no one wanting to be the first to rush to the festive spread. It only took a quick tease from Mist about removing the food to send guests jumping to their feet. One by one, group by group, they moved along the buffet, loading plates with the exquisite Christmas Eve meal that the Moonglow Café and Timberton Hotel had become known for.

"It just gets better every year," Nigel said as he took a seat at a table with Luisa and Rafael. He looked up to see Michael approaching. "Isn't that right, Michael?"

"I must say I agree," Michael said, sliding into an empty seat, a full plate in his hands. He set the plate down and reached for a basket of rolls, offering them to others before taking one for himself. "Maybe you'll return next year," he said to Luisa and Rafael. "Several of us do."

"I can see why," Rafael said. "This meal itself would bring me back."

"It's different every year," Nigel noted. "You should have seen the *buche de noel* we had for dessert one year. It was magnificent."

"I love the decorations," Luisa said. "I wouldn't have thought to fill jars with candy for a centerpiece, but with the candlelight reflecting off the glass, it's delightful."

"Plus later you can eat the candy," Maria said. "It's a decoration and a dessert!" She sat one table away from her mother, Keira by her side.

"You can only eat the candy inside," Keira said, inspecting a jar closely. "The outside has glitter on it, so we can't eat the candy on top by the ribbons."

"A wise decision," Mist said as she passed by with a pitcher of water.

Heather, seated not far away with Liam, Matthew and Olga, looked at Mist and smiled. The girls had been whispering back and forth all day, and Mist had suggested letting them have their own table. It had made sense for them to eat together, and the two-top was situated perfectly to accommodate Maria's wheelchair.

Most townsfolk sat together, but mingled verbally with hotel guests nearby, as well as during trips to the buffet, of which there were many. Although the café featured multiple tables of varying sizes, it was as if the room became one large seating area with no division at all.

As plates were cleared, red crystal goblets of gelato began to emerge, each garnished with mint leaves and a miniature candy cane. Matthew and Liam declined, excusing themselves to prepare for the show. Matthew patted his stomach, citing the need to keep his youthful figure, which brought a round of laughter.

Liam did the same, resulting in more eye-rolling than snickers. Keira stood as well, beckoning to Maria.

"I'm going with Keira," Maria said to her mother as she positioning her hands to turn her chair's wheels."

"I don't know," Luisa said. "Keira needs to get ready for her performance. Why don't you stay with us and have dessert?"

Mist watched from the kitchen doorway, concerned as Maria's face started to cloud over. Fortunately, Rafael spoke up just as Mist was about to intercede.

"Maybe we should let her go, Luisa," Rafael said. "Who knows when she'll have another chance to be backstage at a show?"

"Please?" Maria begged.

Betty, gelato-laden crystal in each hand, leaned toward Mist. "My, the poor girl really looks worried," she whispered.

"It will be fine," Mist said, reassured now that Maria's father had spoken up. Sure enough, Luisa responded as she trusted she would.

"You're right," Luisa said to Rafael. She then turned to Maria. "Go ahead, Maria. I'll bet being backstage with Keira will be exciting.

"Thanks!" Maria, looking both, relieved and excited, quickly rolled herself back from the table and out of the café. Keira skipped alongside her, and the two disappeared down the hall.

Mist sent a look of gratitude to Rafael and resumed serving dessert. "With or without peppermint schnapps?" she asked each guest as she graced each place setting with the festive crystal. Betty followed with a decanter of the sweet liqueur for those who chose to add it.

"How about peppermint schnapps without gelato?" Clive asked, much to the amusement of those around him.

"Why not?" Betty said. "It's Christmas Eve, after all." She took a cordial glass from a china cabinet in the corner of the room, filled it a quarter full and set it in front of Clive. Several other guests followed Clive's suggestion, most stayed with the planned gelato, and a few opted for only coffee, instead. Clayton, who'd been sitting with Maisie, his parents, and Clay Jr., turned down dessert and coffee altogether and excused himself to go set the lights for the performance.

After twenty minutes sharing stories over dessert and coffee, Clayton passed through the room, whispered to Mist, and then left again. In turn, Mist invited the crowd to move to the front parlor, cautioning them to watch their steps, as the lights would be low. She stood back and watched as guests made their way out of the café and through the entry hall. Taking a deep breath, she closed her eyes and exhaled. *Here we go...*

FOURTEEN

L ow lighting barely illuminated the double row of chairs that had been set in a wide semi-circle against the walls, leaving the rest of the room completely dark. Only the bottom of an arched trellis just inside the door caught a fraction of the faint light.

Two local schoolchildren, dressed in their finest holiday garb, handed out souvenir programs as guests entered, giving strict instructions not to open them until after the show. The directions would have been unnecessary, in any case. The room was far too dark for anyone to read. As it was, those attending the show had to inch sideways cautiously as they sought places to sit along the rows. More than a few clinks and groans pierced the air as people bumped into chair legs or stepped on the toes of others close in line.

"How did Clayton manage to make the room this dark?" Betty whispered as she and Mist stood to the side of the door, watching the crowd ease into the parlor. "I can't even see the Christmas tree by the front window. Usually the moonlight outside outlines it, even with no lights on at all."

Mist leaned closer to Betty. "The tree has been moved to the center of the room. The furniture that is usually in front of the fireplace has been moved out.

Only the tree is there. Fortunately the empty fireplace allowed room for the tree to back up close to the wall. We also covered the front window with dark cloth."

"Ah, I understand," Betty said. "And the lighting right now?"

"Two soft lights, aimed only at the chairs," Mist said. Looking around the room, she was impressed with the effort Clayton and his crew had put in. The normally bright front parlor looked indeed like a darkened theatre.

Luisa and Rafael held back, allowing others to file into the rows first, and then took two end seats. Even with the added arch inside the doorway, the entry was wide enough for Maria to sit with them when the show started. Her wheelchair would fit nicely along the edge of the row.

Hushed voices conversed with one another in the manner common to audiences waiting for a show to begin. Paper fluttered as programs settled into laps. Olga took the third seat over in the front row, next to Luisa and Rafael on one side and the professor on the other. Michael took an end seat across the aisle, so that Mist could stand beside him while still attending to the show.

Luisa shuffled nervously in her seat, worried that Maria was going to miss the show. Rafael patted her arm, assuring her that Maria wouldn't miss it, whether she watched from the audience or backstage.

What little light there was faded to black, and the room fell silent. The sound of shuffling feet accompanied faint shadows of moving figures.

When the movement ceased, a stick tapped on wood, replicating the sound of a conductor readying an orchestra.

"Nice touch," Michael whispered to Mist, who simply smiled.

Gradually, a circle of light appeared at the top of the Christmas tree, growing wider and lower as the well-known Tchaikovsky score filled the air. As the illumination reached the floor, two sights brought "oohs" and "aahs" from the audience: a silver box adorned with bright red ribbon just below the lowest branch, and the sleeping figure of Clara curled up beside the tree.

"Look how lovely Keira's costume is," Luisa whispered to Rafael. Mist, overhearing, had to agree. It had only taken a few yards of blue ribbon and white lace to turn the vintage white nightgown from the thrift shop into the proper attire for Clara's dream sequence. In addition, with the young girl's back to the audience, matching blue ribbons and golden ringlets could be seen cascading across her shoulders to match the costume, just as Glenda from the Curl 'N Cue had arranged backstage.

A crescendo of music accompanied a shift of lighting to highlight Matthew, dressed as Herr Drosselmeyer, entering the stage area. His salt-and-pepper hair was a perfect match to his old-fashioned black and white costume, complete with cape and eye patch.

"He's scary!" a young boy near Mist murmured.

"It's okay," Mist said, reassuring the child. "He's really very nice."

Matthew ambled dramatically around the stage with adept footing and sweeping arm movements, finally pausing by the tree to pick up the silver package. With one sideways whoosh of an arm, he pulled the red ribbon off the box, tossing it gleefully to the side. The lid tumbled off along with it, and Matthew reached inside and lifted out the hidden gift: a brightly painted nutcracker. Facing the audience, he held the colorful wooden toy out for all to see.

Again the light shifted, this time highlighting Liam, whose burgundy and gold costume far outshined that of the elderly, eccentric Drosselmeyer. A round of applause circled the room as the handsome Cavalier executed a leap – modified for the limited space – and stepped to the center of the stage.

"Why is the Cavalier appearing so early?" Heather said, being all too familiar with the usual order of the two act ballet. Mist watched her lean forward, taking in all aspects of the scene – the festive tree, the open gift, Herr Drosselmeyer, the Cavalier, and Clara.

Betty, within hearing distance, answered Heather. "It's just an abbreviated show."

"You'll see," Mist added.

The music segued from that of Liam's majestic entrance to a softer portion of the Act I score. Matthew mimed a desire to give the nutcracker gift to the sleeping Clara, imploring the Cavalier's help. Liam spread his arms open and bowed his head in understanding, then tiptoed gracefully around Clara so that he faced the audience. Lowering to one knee to the floor, he gently slid both arms under the sleeping girl and raised her from the floor.

"No, it can't be!" Luisa gasped, both hands flying to her mouth. Rafael wrapped his arm around her to calm her. Others in the audience began to whisper as they caught on.

Liam turned a full circle as the waking Clara's arms began to stretch. He then carefully adjusted her position so that he held her legs curled inside one arm, and supported her ribcage with the other. Now, with the audience's full view of the sweet face beneath the golden curls and blue ribbon, it was clear that Clara was not Keira, but Marie.

Matthew stepped forward and bowed, then presented Clara with the nutcracker. As he stepped back, Marie clasped the new gift with both hands and held it high in the air, Liam swinging her gently forward to help extend her reach.

Suddenly the arch by the entry way lit up with twinkling lights intertwined with white cotton batting. Glittery paper snowflakes hung from the top of the arch, as well as from the ceiling above. The Cavalier moved swiftly to the arch, Clara secure in his arms.

"The Land of Snow!" one guest murmured as Liam spun Marie in circles below the twinkling lights and snowflakes.

As Liam and Marie moved back across the room, another set of sparkling lights came on, resulting in more gasps throughout the room. Herr Drosselmeyer had retreated offstage during the Cavalier and Clara's trip through the Land of Snow, reappearing with her wheelchair, now adorned with strands of twinkling lights and garlands of candy. As Liam placed Marie gently in the chair, she sat upright, as regal as a princess, ready for the show in The Land of Sweets.

A round of applause filled the room, and then faded away as Matthew, Liam and Marie all stayed in character - a sign the performance wasn't over.

Heather leaned forward again, her eyes searching the stage with the unspoken question that had occurred to more than a few in the audience. Olga tapped her cane to get Heather's attention, smiled, and mouthed the words, "Just wait."

The stage area faded to black, and again the audience heard the sound of feet moving in the dark. After a moment of silence, the lights came back on, sudden and bright, this time illuminating the most beautiful Sugar Plum Fairy the audience had ever seen. Keira stood poised in the center of the stage area, her usual white snowflake costume now adorned with pink tulle draped in scalloped fashion from her waistline and shoulder seams. Pink and lavender organza flowers dotted each curve of fabric. A headpiece of pink roses and baby's breath framed a classic hair bun above her slender neck. Mist sent Maisie a smile of appreciation for that final touch.

As the bell-chiming music of the Dance of the Sugar Plum Fairy began, Keira executed precise steps and graceful movements. Each pirouette and every arabesque demonstrated technique far beyond that of a dancer her age. And her glee was contagious when, during a brief pas de deux, Liam lifted her in the air.

"Thank goodness for our high ceilings," Betty said as applause broke out.

Liam lowered Keira effortlessly to the floor, and then stood back, arm extended toward her. Posing with serene preparation, the Sugar Plum Fairy spun into a final series of turns and ended with a crisp finish.

Applause and cheers filled the room and floated throughout the hotel as Keira curtsied to each side, and then extended an arm just as Liam had done. Maria, now unplugged from the source of her chair's twinkling lights, rolled out beside Keira. The two girls hugged, bringing the audience to its feet for a standing ovation. Matthew and Liam walked out to join the girls, placing a bouquet of roses in each dancer's lap and then standing to the each side. All four bowed as guests snapped photos of the proud moment.

After the townsfolk had gone home, the hotel guests had retired for the night, and the furniture had reclaimed its regular placement, Mist, Michael, Betty and Clive sat together in the front parlor. Upstairs, a young dancer dreamed of her reign over the Land of Sweets, dressed in flowing pink and lavender, a halo of roses above her head. Downstairs, another dancer dreamed of soaring through the Land of Snow with her Nutcracker, no longer just a fantasy. And the adults simply sat in silence. After all, for that particular Christmas Eve, everything important had already been said.

FIFTEEN

Sunlight flowed through the windows of the café as guests arrived for the late breakfast that Mist aptly called Christmas Brunch. Serving at the later hours on Christmas Day allowed townsfolk to observe morning traditions with their families before heading over for a casual holiday meal. Hotel guests could ease into the day with coffee and croissants from the lobby, lingering in their rooms a little longer than usual, if they desired to. And quite a few chose to do exactly that, as the activities of the night before had left everyone ready for a good night's sleep, and a leisurely morning.

Mist, however, had stayed up late after everyone retired, as was her habit on Christmas eve. This was the time her paintbrush most inspired her, when she could touch up the departing gifts she traditionally gave guests to take home as mementos of their stay.

"Look at that clever fruit plate!" Luisa commented, noting the holiday colors of the grapes, raspberries, kiwi, strawberries, and green apple slices. "It's like a Christmas mosaic." Rafael, entering with her, smiled, but looked far more interested in the chafing dishes of eggs benedict breakfast casserole and maple-pepper bacon.

"Good morning and Merry Christmas," Mist said as she greeted each guest. Unlike her usual tendency to breeze through the hotel in long skirts, she'd chosen to wear black rayon slacks and an ivory embroidered peasant blouse with gathered neckline and bell sleeves. A triple strand of Moroccan beads accented the outfit. The only nod to holiday colors was a red silk scarf which loosely tied her hair at the nape of her neck.

Betty, on the other hand, was sufficiently decked out for a holiday catalog. Her red skirt grazed the top of gold ankle boots, and her kelly green sweater featured a puffed reindeer design than ran from neckline to waistline. Clip-on earrings shaped like candy canes graced her earlobes. Clive was only slightly less festive in a forest green shirt and red sweater vest.

"I'm too tired to roll myself in," Maria said, yawning dramatically as Keira wheeled her into the room. "So I had to ask the Sugar Plum Fairy to bring me to breakfast."

"You girls were simply brilliant last night," Nigel said. He'd arrived just after Mist opened the café doors. Cup of tea in hand, he sat with Olga at a window table. Keira and Maria stopped by the table and hugged Olga before taking places at the larger table with Luisa and Rafael. Heather also joined the group, sitting down next to Luisa, proud mothers side by side.

"Did you see that?" Betty said to Mist. "Both girls went to greet Olga as soon as they saw her, before even choosing a table or looking at the food."

"Yes," Mist said, smiling. "I suspect Olga has a more interesting background than she's let on. I hope she'll share it with us before she leaves."

"She *has* spent quite a bit of time with the girls the last couple of days, now that I think about it," Betty said.

Clive, to no one's surprise, had been the first to arrive. He sat with Clayton, Maisie, Clay Jr., and Clayton's parents. Matthew and Liam had both joined the table with Nigel and Olga.

Michael entered last, taking a seat at the large table with the others there. He patted the empty seat next to him, motioning for Mist to join group.

"Go on," Betty said, encouraging Mist to sit with the others. "I can watch the buffet, and you deserve to relax and enjoy today." Others at the table also echoed Michael's sentiments, especially Maria and Keira who waved their arms enthusiastically.

Mist tilted her head to the side, as if pondering the idea whimsically. "You know, I think I will," she said, much to everyone's delight.

"Lovely music you have playing this morning," Heather said as Mist sat down. "Carol of the Bells, one of my favorites. And Little Drummer Boy before that."

"A capella, too," Nigel added from the window table. "Pentatonix. I do enjoy their Christmas selections." Heads nodded in agreement as guests took bites of the brunch fare.

Betty slipped a small serving of fruit in front of Mist, so that she'd have something to eat along with the others.

"Is that all you're going to have?" Maria asked.

Mist laughed. "If only you knew how much taste-testing I do while preparing meals."

"Now wait just a minute," Clive said, attempting to pull off a serious objection. "I thought I was the official taste-tester around these parts!"

"You are, dear," Betty said. She placed her hands on his shoulders and kissed the top of his head. "Your reputation for that is well-established."

Clive let out an exaggerated sigh of relief, bringing both laughter and teasing in turn. The cheerful camaraderie continued throughout the meal, after which Mist invited guests to move to the front parlor.

Just as it had in the café, sunlight flowed in from outside as guests gathered in the main room to enjoy the beautifully decorated Christmas tree, a warm fire in the fireplace, and each other's company. Perry Como's smooth voice began telling everyone it was "beginning to look a lot like Christmas," which, indeed, it was. Clive escorted Betty over to the tree and asked her to close her eyes while he pulled a "surprise" from one of the back branches – a silver ornament that he handcrafted for her each year, this time a reindeer. Tiny blue Yogo sapphires sparkled from an etched scarf around the reindeer's neck.

"It's beautiful, Clive!" Betty exclaimed, holding the twinkling ornament in the sunlight. She hung it on a front branch and gave Clive an affectionate hug.

Marie's parents pulled out gifts of clothing and books that they'd brought, but kept hidden. Heather did the same, giving Keira a gold ballet shoe pendant, along with a chiffon ballet wrap skirt. The other adults watched the children open their gifts, smiling and remembering the excitement of their own childhoods.

Mist moved to the Christmas tree and reached between branches, slowly pulling out small squares of fabric tied with raffia. "I have something for each of you, so you can remember spending this holiday here with us." She handed each guest one of the fabric squares.

"I don't think it's possible to forget Christmas at The Timberton Hotel, Mist," Michael said as he leaned back in his favorite chair.

"Exactly right," Nigel said. "Each year here creates a lasting memory." Luisa and Rafael agreed it would be a holiday to remember for years to come. Heather, Matthew and Liam expressed the same sentiments. The girls, caught up in showing each other their gifts, were oblivious to the adult discussion.

Mist watched as each person pulled the raffia, letting the cloth fall to the floor, revealing a miniature painting. Smiles on the already cheerful crowd widened.

"It's me as Clara!" Marie said, holding up the painting, which replicated her raising the nutcracker high in the air.

"Or as Marie," Olga pointed out. "Clara, Marie, Masha, even. All those names have been used in different versions over the years."

Marie nodded, remembering that her name was the one used in the original story by E.T.A. Hoffman. "I love it!"

"Same here," Keira said, showing her painting to everyone. "I'm in my Sugar Plum Fairy outfit! Thank you, Mist!" She jumped up and ran to Mist, wrapping her arms around her. Marie did the same.

Matthew and Liam sighed at the sight of theirs, a painting of the hotel itself, but with the hotel sign changed to read "Theatre."

"So that you can remember you had a place to go when you lost your theatre," Mist said. "A place to call home for the holidays - a place privileged to have you here with us."

Michael smiled as he held his painting up quietly so that Mist could see that he received it. Contrary to the sentimental paintings some were receiving, his was a winding road with Timberton on one end and Missoula on the other. He winked at Mist, and she blushed. Nothing could have pleased them more than their closer proximity to each other.

"Show us yours," both girls said to their parents. Luisa, Rafael and Heather held theirs up. Each painting showed the two girls together at the end of the show, in costume, holding their bouquets with expressions of joy.

"These are wonderful, Mist," Luisa said. "There's nothing like seeing your child happy, especially when it involves a dream coming true." Rafael nodded.

"I feel the same way," Heather said. "Keira dreams of being the Sugar Plum Fairy someday. Now she's had a chance, thanks to you. It seems you pull off miracles here, Mist."

"She does," Michael said. "I've watched for several years now."

"We all work together to create miracles in our lives," Mist said. "And sometimes …" she paused to direct her attention to the one person who had yet to show her painting. "Sometimes we have a little extra magic show up when we least expect it."

Heads turned, finally landing on Olga, who tapped her cane and looked at everyone.

"Show us your picture, Olga," Keira said.

"Yes, show us," Maria echoed.

Olga set her cane aside and showed the painting of an old building with eight columns across the front, a bouquet of flowers on the steps. "How did you know?" she asked Mist.

Mist smiled. "The way you touched Keira's wrist outside when the girls were practicing arm movements, your knowledge of the Nutcracker history, your birthplace of St. Petersburg, and the trip to the library with the girls and Liam, which gave you space to rehearse the surprise without others knowing."

"She helped with the Sugar Plum steps. She knew them all!" Keira said proudly, and then looked closer at Olga's painting. "What is that building?"

"It is the Bolshoi Theatre, in Moscow" Olga said. "A magnificent building. I spent many years performing there under Yuri Grigorovich. He set our version of The Nutcracker in 1966."

"Oh, you were the original Sugar Plum Fairy!" Keira said.

Olga laughed, the first time anyone had seen her relax her regal composure. "Oh, no, certainly not. There were many Sugar Plum Fairies before me, and many after. And there will be many more. I believe I just saw a beautiful one last night."

"The flowers on the steps are for your contribution to last night," Mist said. "You really helped dreams come true for two young dancers."

"Just as you make dreams come true here, Mist," Betty said. "In the hotel, as well as the Moonglow Café."

"As they say, it takes a village," Mist said. "Meanwhile, it's a lovely day outside. I encourage you all to enjoy it. Or stay by the fire and read. Or simply listen to the music."

Some guests chose to bundle up and go outside, others lingered in the parlor. The girls headed out to build a "snow dancer," as they called it. Betty and Clive retired to the kitchen to relax and enjoy a cup of coffee together.

Mist grabbed a shawl and walked out to the front porch, Michael alongside.

"Every Christmas is certainly an adventure here," Michael said.

"Not only Christmas, but every day, everywhere" Mist said. "Adventure is always around us if we choose to see it." Michael wrapped his arms around her and gently pulled her close.

"That means throughout the year," Michael pointed out.

"Yes, it does." Mist smiled.

"So I'll see you more this year," Michael said, kissing her neck softly on one side.

"Yes, I believe so." An impish expression crossed her face. "Only because Missoula is much closer than

LSU, where you were teaching before. That's the only reason. Convenience."

"I see. Well, I knew that." Michael kissed her neck again, this time on the other side. "Oh, I almost forgot," he said, teasing. He reached into a pocket and pulled out a beautiful gold chain. "We'll pick something out together to put on this chain when you come up to the art exhibit, something that speaks to that spirit of yours."

"How perfect." Mist said. "You see? They are everywhere, adventures."

"And many more to come," Michael said.

Mist touched the chain around her neck and smiled. "Yes, many more to come."

BETTY'S COOKIE EXCHANGE RECIPES

Glazed Cinnamon Nuts
Christmas Crack
White Christmas Fudge
Cathedral Cookies
Molasses Sugar Cookies
Peanut Butter Fudge
Lemon Crinkles
Krum Kake Cookies
Cranberry Drop Cookies
Double Chocolate Walnut Brownies
Granny's Butter Rolls
Christmas Hard Candy
Lingonberry Macarons
Lingonberry Buttercream Filling
Yummy Dates
Twenty-First Century Peanut Brittle
Healthy No-Bake Apple Energy Bites
Grandma Chauncey's Date Nut Bars
No-Bake Peanut Butter Oatmeal Cookies
Cinnamon Refrigerator Cookies
Mocha Candied Nuts
All-in-One-Pan Cookies
Date Balls
Applesauce Cookies
Thimble Cookies

Glazed Cinnamon Nuts

(A family recipe)

Ingredients:

1 cup sugar
1/4 cup water
1/8 teaspoon cream of tartar
Heaping teaspoon of cinnamon
1 tablespoon butter
1 1/2 cups walnut halves

Directions:

Boil sugar, water, cream of tartar and cinnamon to soft ball stage (236 degrees.)

Remove from heat.

Add butter and walnuts.

Stir until walnuts separate.

Place on wax paper to cool.

CHRISTMAS CRACK
(Submitted by Kim Davis)

Ingredients

1-1/4 sleeves saltine crackers (about 50 crackers)
1 cup butter
1 cup brown sugar
1 (12-ounce) package chocolate chips (milk, semi-sweet, or dark)
1 (8-ounce) package toffee pieces

Instructions

Preheat oven to 400 degrees (F)

Line a baking sheet with foil.

Lay the saltine crackers on the baking sheet, arranging so no space remains between the crackers. It's okay to break the crackers into pieces to fit as needed.

Melt the butter in a medium-sized saucepan over medium heat then add the sugar and stir until it dissolves. Bring to a boil then reduce the heat to medium-low and boil for 4 minutes.

Immediately pour over the saltine crackers and using a spatula, make sure all the crackers are covered with the mixture.

Bake for 7 - 9 minutes, or until bubbly. Remove from the oven and sprinkle the chocolate chips over the top and return to the oven for 1 minute.

Remove from the oven and using a spatula, spread the chocolate over the tops of the crackers. Make sure the chocolate covers the entire surface.

Sprinkle the toffee pieces over the top of the melted chocolate.

Cool to room temperature for 30 minutes then place in the refrigerator for 30 - 60 minutes, or until the chocolate is firm.

Remove the Christmas Crack from the pan and break into pieces.

Store in an airtight container for up to two weeks.

WHITE CHRISTMAS FUDGE
(Submitted by Jean Daniel)

Ingredients:

2 1/2 cups granulated sugar
1/2 cup sour cream
1/4 cup milk
2 tablespoons butter
1 tablespoon light corn syrup
1/4 teaspoon salt
2 teaspoons vanilla
1 cup quartered candied cherries
1 cup chopped walnuts (could also use pecans)

Directions:

Combine sugar, sour cream, milk, butter, corn syrup and salt in heavy saucepan. Stir on moderate heat until the sugar completely dissolves, and mixture reaches boil.

Boil over medium heat 9-10 minutes or until it reaches 238 on candy thermometer. Remove from heat and allow to stand for an hour. It should reach at least 110 before you add the vanilla.

Beat until the mixture loses its gloss, which may take a little bit and some elbow grease but it will get there.

Stir in cherries and the nuts. Pat into a buttered pan. Cut into squares.

CATHEDRAL COOKIES
(Submitted by Teri Fish)

Ingredients:

½ cup butter
1 (16 ounce) package milk chocolate chips
1 teaspoon vanilla extract
1 cup chopped walnuts (optional)
1 (16 ounce) package colored miniature marshmallows
2 cups flaked coconut

Directions:

Melt butter and chocolate chips in heavy saucepan over medium heat; mix until smooth and creamy; remove from heat and stir in the vanilla. Fold in marshmallows and walnuts.

Scatter about half of the coconut onto a large baking sheet lined with wax paper. Pour the mixture into log on the coconut lined wax paper pour more coconut on top of it and with the wax paper roll the mixture into a log. Refrigerate until log is firm, about 1 hour.

Cut log into ¾ inch slices. Keep refrigerated to keep from melting.

Option: You can also microwave chocolate chips for 30 seconds on high then add butter and microwave in 30 second increments until smooth. Then add vanilla, marshmallows and nuts.

If you don't like or can't use coconut you can use powdered sugar. I have poured chocolate mixture onto wax paper rolled into log and then sprinkled powdered sugar over all sides.

Molasses Sugar Cookies
(Submitted by Bea Tackett)

Ingredients:

3/4 cup shortening
1 cup sugar
1/4 cup molasses
1 egg
2 teaspoon baking soda
2 cups flour
1/4 teaspoon cloves
1/2 teaspoon ginger
1 teaspoon cinnamon
1/2 teaspoon salt

Directions:

Melt shortening in a saucepan over low heat. Remove from heat; let cool.

Add sugar, molasses and egg; beat well.

Sift together flour, salt, and spices. Add to first mixture; mix well.

Form into 1" balls; roll in sugar and place on greased cookie sheet, 2" apart.

Bake at 375 degrees for 8-10 minutes.

PEANUT BUTTER FUDGE
(Submitted by Petrenia Snodgrass Etheridge)

Ingredients:

1 bag of peanut butter chips
1 tub of milk chocolate cake icing.

Directions:

Melt peanut butter chips in microwave or double boiler.

Gradually stir in icing and pour into 9x9 baking dish.

Allow to set for several hours and cut into squares.

Note: Use chocolate chips for regular fudge, or add pecans or walnuts for variety.

LEMON CRINKLES
(Submitted by Kim Davis)

Ingredients:

1/2 cup unsalted butter, room temperature
1 cup (7.1 ounces) granulated sugar
1 egg, room temperature
1/2 teaspoon vanilla extract
1/2 to 1 teaspoon lemon extract, depending on how lemony you want
1 teaspoon lemon zest
1 tablespoon fresh lemon juice
1-1/2 cups (7.2 ounces) all-purpose flour
1/2 teaspoon salt
1/4 teaspoon baking powder
1/4 teaspoon baking soda
1/2 cup granulated sugar (for rolling dough)

Directions:

Don't preheat the oven yet. The cookie dough will need to chill first.

Line baking sheet with parchment paper and set aside.

In a medium-sized bowl, whisk together the flour, salt, baking powder, and baking soda. Set aside.

In the bowl of a standing mixer, whip the butter and granulated sugar together until fluffy, about 2 minutes on medium speed.

Add the egg and beat until fully incorporated.

Mix in the vanilla, lemon extract, lemon zest, and lemon juice.

With the mixer running on lowest speed, slowly add the flour mixture. Beat just until it is fully incorporated.

Cover the cookie dough with plastic wrap and allow to chill in the refrigerator for 1 hour or even overnight.

Preheat oven to 350 degrees (F).

Place remaining 1/2 cup granulated sugar in a shallow bowl.

Form cookie dough into small balls, about a heaping teaspoon.

Roll the balls in the granulated sugar and place on the parchment-lined baking sheet, at least 2 inches apart. Don't crowd the cookies as they spread. You should have 12 cookies per baking sheet.

Bake for 9 to 11 minutes. The edges should just be turning light golden and the tops should be crackled.

Remove from the oven and allow to cool on the baking sheet for 5 minutes before transferring to a wire cooling rack.

Cool completely and store leftovers in an airtight container at room temperature for up to 3 days.

Notes:

These cookies are ideal for making ahead of time and freezing for spur-of-the-moment freshly-baked cookies! Simply roll the dough balls in the sugar, then freeze them on a parchment-lined baking sheet. When solid, transfer the dough to a freezer-safe ziplock bag. When ready to bake, place the dough on a parchment-lined baking sheet and allow to sit at room temperature while pre-heating the oven. You may need to bake an additional minute, depending on how chilled the dough is when you start baking.

Makes 30 - 40 cookies depending on size.

Krum Kake Cookies
(Submitted by Lynette Ausland Eads)

Ingredients:

1 cup sugar
½ cup melted butter (or oleo)
½ teaspoon vanilla flavoring
3 eggs
½ cup whipping cream
2 cups flour
1 teaspoon nutmeg
½ to 1 teaspoon cardamom

Directions:

Beat cream and set aside. Beat eggs until very light, then add sugar, spices, melted butter, cream, & flavoring. May add almond or lemon flavoring instead of vanilla. Stir in flour.

Heat Krumkake iron on medium heat on stove top. Put a teaspoonful of batter on the iron. Close the iron, and bake one minute or less, turn iron over and bake until lightly browned. Remove cookie from iron and quickly roll on cone – shape form. Store in air tight container.

Notes:

Enjoy plain or filled with whipped cream.

CRANBERRY DROP COOKIES
(Submitted by Jan Knight)

Ingredients:

1/2 cup butter, softened
1 cup sugar
3/4 cup brown sugar
1/4 cup milk
2 tablespoons orange juice plus the zest of 1 orange
2 1/3 cup flour
1 teaspoon baking powder
1/4 teaspoon baking soda
1/2 teaspoon salt
1 cup chopped walnuts
2 1/2 cups coarsely chopped cranberries

Directions:

Wash cranberries in sieve. Drain on paper towels.

Cream butter & sugars. Beat in milk, orange juice, & egg.

Blend dry ingredients with whisk in a separate bowl. Add to mixture. Stir in nuts, cranberries, & orange zest.

Drop by teaspoonful onto nonstick baking sheet or parchment paper.

Bake at 350 degrees for approximately 12 minutes or until light brown. Let cool.

Option: Finish with a powdered sugar glaze tinted pink for a festive touch! Keep in a single layer in storage container.

DOUBLE CHOCOLATE WALNUT BROWNIES
(Submitted by Valerie Peterson)

Ingredients:

1 cup butter or margarine
4 sq. unsweetened chocolate
2 cups sugar
3 eggs
1 teaspoon vanilla
1 cup sifted flour
1 ½ cups coarsely chopped walnuts
1 package chocolate chips

Directions:

Melt butter and chocolate together.

Stir in sugar, eggs, and vanilla.

Add flour and mix well.

Pour into greased 9 x 13 pan.

Sprinkle with nuts and chocolate chips

Bake at 350 degrees for 35minutes.

GRANNY'S BUTTER ROLLS
(Submitted by Petrenia Snodgrass Etheridge)

Ingredients:

2 cups sugar
3 cups milk
2 teaspoons vanilla
2 cups flour
1 cup shortening
2/3 cup milk
1 or 2 sticks margarine

Directions:

Mix 3 cups milk, vanilla, and sugar and bring to a boil.

Knead flour and enough milk and shortening to make dough, as if making biscuits.

Roll out dough on cooking sheet or foil until it's thin.

Spread margarine with knife all over dough and sprinkle with sugar.

Roll dough up into a roll and cut in about 2-inch pieces.

Drop in milk mixture in deep casserole dish.

Bake at 350 degrees until rolls are brown.

Christmas Hard Candy
(Submitted by Betty Escobar)

Ingredients:

3 ½ cups sugar
1 cup light corn syrup
1 cup water
¼ - ½ teaspoon cinnamon or peppermint oil
1 teaspoon red or green food coloring

Directions:

In a large heavy saucepan, combine sugar, corn syrup and water.

Cook on medium-high heat until candy thermometer reaches 300 degrees (hard-crack stage,) stirring occasionally.

Remove from the heat. Stir in oil and food coloring, keeping away from face, as odor is very strong.

Immediately pour onto a greased cookie sheet. Cool and break into pieces. Store in airtight containers.

LINGONBERRY MACARONS

(Submitted by Lisa Maliga, from her book, *Baking Macarons: The Swiss Meringue Method*)

Ingredients:

160 grams powdered sugar, sift with almond flour
160 grams almond flour, sift with powdered sugar
150 grams egg whites
180 grams confectioners' sugar, sieved
1 tablespoon [8 grams] arrowroot powder
1/2 teaspoon [3 grams] cream of tartar
Purple or pink food gel color

Directions:

Preheat oven to 300 Fahrenheit/150 Celsius.

Sift the almond flour and confectioners' sugar together into a bowl. Stir in the arrowroot powder and set aside.

Put a template on a baking sheet and place a silicone mat or parchment paper over it. Set aside.

In the bowl of a stand mixer, add egg whites and confectioners' sugar. Whisk until well combined. Place bowl over steaming pot with just enough water, as you don't want the water touching the bowl. Heat on medium heat until it steams. Test to make sure it's hot enough by sticking your clean finger in the meringue near the center of the bowl. If using a candy thermometer the temperature should be about 130 F [54 C]. Remove from heat and place bowl back onto stand mixer.

Add the cream of tartar. Whisk on medium to high speed until firm peaks form. Egg whites should be glossy and if you flip the bowl upside down, nothing will come out.

Add food coloring and whisk until the color is incorporated.

Remove the whisk and add the paddle attachment [if using one].

Add the presifted almond flour and confectioners' sugar mixture.

Turn mixer to low or medium speed and mix for up to 10 seconds. If that doesn't mix the batter thoroughly, mix for another 10 seconds. Turn off mixer and with your spatula, run it around the sides and bottom of bowl to make sure all the dry ingredients are incorporated. Test for the ribbon stage. When you lift your spatula above the bowl, the batter should fall back to the bowl as one continuous stream and create a ribbon pattern.

Pour batter into a large pastry bag fitted with a large round tip. Pipe onto the silicone or parchment covered baking sheets. When finished with each sheet, bang baking sheet on counter to remove air bubbles. If you see any air bubbles, pop them with a toothpick.

Let shells rest on a flat surface in a cool, dry area for about 30 minutes. The surface will change from glossy to matte. To make sure they're done, gently touch the edge of one with your finger. There should be no trace of batter on your finger.

Bake for 15-20 minutes. This will vary depending on your oven. Carefully monitor the baking process and check your oven thermometer. After 8 or so minutes, rotate the tray to ensure even baking.

Macarons are done when you peel back the mat or the parchment paper and the shells don't stick.

Remove from oven and gently slide the parchment or silicone mat onto a cooling rack. The shells should be cool enough to remove after 10 minutes.

Place macaron shells on a wax paper covered baking sheet or tray for filling. Match similar sized shells together. Pipe the filling on the flat side of one shell and gently place the second shell on top.

Notes:
Lingonberries are tart like cranberries. They make a lovely contrast to sweet macaron shells.

LINGONBERRY BUTTERCREAM FILLING

(Submitted by Lisa Maliga, from her book,
Baking Macarons: The Swiss Meringue Method)

Ingredients:

Lingonberry jam, strained
220 grams [2 cups] confectioners' sugar, sifted
1 teaspoon vanilla
Burgundy gel food colorant

Directions:

Add the butter to the bowl of a stand mixer and mix until creamy.

Add the strained lingonberry jam, followed by the confectioners' sugar.

Mix on high speed for several minutes.

Spoon into a piping bag with a round or star-shaped tip.

YUMMY DATES
(Submitted by Deb Kenyon Thom)

Ingredients:

Large fresh dates
English walnuts
Powdered sugar

Directions:

Slice open a large fresh date and remove the seed.

Insert half of an English walnut.

Pinch date closed and roll in powdered sugar.

TWENTY-FIRST CENTURY PEANUT BRITTLE
(Submitted by Deb Kenyon Thom)

Ingredients:

1 cup white sugar
1/2 cup light corn syrup
1 cup raw peanuts
1/2 teaspoon salt
1 teaspoon butter
1 teaspoon vanilla
1 teaspoon baking soda

Directions:

Grease a large cookie sheet.

Using a large microwaveable bowl, mix sugar and syrup together. Heat in a microwave oven on high for three minutes.

Add peanuts and salt, stir then heat in a microwave oven for three more minutes.

Add butter and vanilla, stir and heat in a microwave oven for two or three minutes.

Remove from the microwave, add baking soda and stir well. It will get foamy. Immediately pour onto your buttered cookie sheet pan and spread it out with your spoon.

Let the candy cool and whack on the counter top or sturdy table to release candy from the pan.

HEALTHY NO-BAKE APPLE ENERGY BITES

(Submitted by Lori Sparks Shoemake, from her blog *50 with Flair* - www.50withflair.com)

Ingredients:

1-1/2 cups quick or old-fashioned oats (not instant)
3/4 cup creamy peanut butter, I use a natural type
3/4 cup grated apple
1/2 cup chopped pecans (or your choice of chopped nut)
1/3 cup ground flax seed (or flax seed meal)
1/3 cup honey
2 tablespoons sesame seeds (or your choice of small seeds)
1/2 teaspoon vanilla extract
1/2 teaspoon cinnamon (or ginger for some "bite", or cinnamon-ginger combination)

Directions:

Stir all ingredients together in a bowl until completely combined; extra oats can be added if the mixture seems too soft and sticky. Cover and chill in refrigerator for 30 minutes until firm. Then roll the mixture into 1-inch balls which should yield 18-20 bites. Store in an airtight container in the refrigerator for up to one week, if they last that long! Enjoy!

Tip: dampening your fingers/hands with a bit of water will keep the mixture from sticking to your hands too much

Notes:
45 minutes total time is 15 minutes prep, plus 30 minutes of chill time for the bites to firm up.
Try adding your favorite nuts, dried fruits or even protein powder, etc.

Grandma Chauncey's Date Nut Bars
(Submitted by Taryn Lee)

Ingredients:

1/4 cup oil
1 cup brown sugar
2 eggs
1/2 teaspoon vanilla
1/4 teaspoon ginger
3/4 cup flour
1/2 cup chopped pecans or walnuts
1 cup finely, chopped dates
Powdered sugar (to roll bars in)

Directions:

Mix oil and brown sugar. Add eggs and vanilla; beat well.

Add all dry ingredients except powdered sugar and stir well.

Put mixture into oiled 8X8 inch pan.

Bake at 350 degrees for 30 to 35 minutes.

Cut into bars and roll in powdered sugar.

NO-BAKE PEANUT BUTTER OATMEAL COOKIES
(Submitted by Betty Escobar)

Ingredients:

2 cups sugar
1/2 cup milk
4 tablespoons cocoa
3/4 stick butter
½ cup peanut butter
2 cups quick oats

Directions:

Bring to rolling boil and cook for 1 minute.

Take off heat and add 1/2 cup peanut butter and 1 teaspoon vanilla.

Stir until peanut butter is mixed in well, and then add 2 cups quick oats.

Form into balls or cookies of desired shape.

CINNAMON REFRIGERATOR COOKIES
(Submitted by Robyn Seitzer)

Ingredients:

3 ½ cups flour
1 teaspoon baking soda
1 tablespoon cinnamon
¼ teaspoon salt
1 cup shortening
1 cup brown sugar
1 cup white sugar
2 eggs
1 cup chopped nuts or raisins (optional)

Directions:

Combine flour, soda, cinnamon and salt. Set aside.

Cream shortening and sugars. Beat eggs until light then mix with creamed mixture.

Add dry ingredients 1/3rd at a time, beating after each addition. Add optional ingredients if desired.

Divide dough into two and roll into log until about two inches in diameter. Loosely wrap in waxed paper and refrigerate approx. one hour.

Pre-heat oven to 350. Slice and bake 7 to 10 minutes.

MOCHA CANDIED NUTS
(Submitted by Kathleen Brown)

Ingredients:

1-1/2 cups sugar (beet)
1 tablespoon corn syrup
1/2 cup warm, strong coffee (or 1 tablespoon instant coffee +
1/2 cup water)
2-1/2 cups walnuts, pecans, or other nuts

Directions:

Blend together in a saucepan the sugar, corn syrup, and coffee.

Cook to softball stage (240 degrees Fahrenheit,) about 4 minutes.

Remove from heat and add the nuts. Stir until creamy.

Turn onto a greased cookie sheet or waxed paper; separate nuts
with 2 forks. Let cool.

All-In-One-Pan Cookies
(Submitted by Kathleen Brown)

Ingredients:

1/2 cup butter or margarine
1 cup crushed graham crackers
1 cup coconut
1 cup chocolate chips
1 cup chopped nuts
1 can (14 oz.) sweetened condensed milk

Directions:

Melt butter in 9" x 13" pan.

Add graham crackers to butter.

Sprinkle on coconut, chocolate chips, and nuts.

Drizzle on sweetened condensed milk.

Bake at 350 degrees for 20-25 minutes. Cut into squares.

DATE BALLS
(Submitted by Vera Kenyon)

Ingredients:

8 oz. package of dates, chopped
2 eggs, lightly beaten
1 stick of butter
1 cup of chopped nuts
2 teaspoons of vanilla
2 cups of crispy rice cereal 2+ cups of flaked, sweetened coconut
(for rolling the date balls)

Directions:

Melt the butter over low heat. Don't let it get too hot.

Whisk in the dates, eggs and vanilla. Stir well. Cook for approximately five minutes.

Add in the nuts and crispy rice cereal. Mix well.

While the mixture is still warm form into small balls and then roll in coconut. Work fast. Let cool.

Freezes well so you can make these up ahead of the holiday.

APPLESAUCE COOKIES
(Submitted by Valerie Peterson)

Ingredients:

½ cup butter
½ cup brown sugar
½ cup sugar
1 egg
1 teaspoon baking soda
1 cup applesauce
2 cups flour
½ teaspoon cloves
½ teaspoon salt
½ teaspoon cinnamon
1 teaspoon nutmeg

Directions:

Cream butter, sugar and egg.

Add baking soda and applesauce.

Mix dry ingredients together and add to wet ingredients.

Drop onto greased cookie sheet and bake at 425 degrees for 8-10 minutes.

Thimble Cookies
(Submitted by Valerie Peterson)

Ingredients:

1 cup butter
1 cup brown sugar
1 egg yolk
1 teaspoon vanilla
2 cups sifted flour
Egg white as needed, unbeaten
Cherries
Chopped nuts

Directions:

Mix all ingredients except cherries and nuts together.

Roll into balls the size of a walnut and dip in unbeaten egg white.

Dip in chopped nuts and press a half cherry into each center.

Bake at 350 degrees for approx. 10 minutes.

Makes about 6 dozen.

Option: Use jelly instead of cherries

ACKNOWLEDGEMENTS

The characters in the Moonglow Christmas series may tell the stories of their holidays at the Timberton Hotel, but not without help. There is a great team behind the scenes, and everyone in it deserves a round of applause. D.A. Sarac at The Editing Pen provided the much-needed polishing to make this story shine on the inside. Keri Knutson of Alchemy Book Covers matched that shine on the outside with her exquisite cover design. Formatting help varies from book to book, and from digital to print, inevitably falling on a few of the following shoulders: Tim Renfrow, Richard Houston, Tara Meyers, Aaron Linsdau, and Normarie Lego. Heartfelt gratitude is always well-earned by beta readers Jay Garner, Louise Martens, Karen Putnam, and Carol Anderson. And if there's such a thing as a "beta listener," that credit goes to Paul Sterrett, for listening day in and day out as the stories develop.

This year's tantalizing recipes in the back of the book were generously provided by Kim Davis, Jean Daniel, Teri Fish, Bea Tackett, Petrenia Snodgrass Etheridge, Lynette Ausland Eads, Jan Knight, Valerie Peterson, Betty Escobar, Lisa Maliga, Deb Kenyon Thom, Lori Sparks Shoemake, Taryn Lee, Robin Seitzer, Kathleen Brown, and Vera Kenyon. Time to get out the bowls and baking utensils and enjoy the treats they've shared!

RECIPE NOTES

RECIPE NOTES

Recipe Notes

RECIPE NOTES

RECIPE NOTES

RECIPE NOTES

RECIPE NOTES

www.ingramcontent.com/pod-product-compliance
Lightning Source LLC
Chambersburg PA
CBHW021022120726
47905CB00009B/3129